D0055346

GWENDOLEN GROSS

"Her deceptively spare style glistens."
—*Publishers Weekly*

———

Praise for her lyrical, compulsively readable novels

WHEN SHE WAS GONE

"What happens behind the closed doors of a neighborhood, and beyond the facades of the people who live there? Gwendolen Gross has the sharp insight of the documentarian, turning her lens on each house of a frightened town after a college-bound girl goes missing. Full of heart but free of sentimentality, *When She Was Gone* shows the sinews of belonging and not-belonging that bind a community."

—Nichole Bernier, author of
The Unfinished Work of Elizabeth D

"Gwendolen Gross uses the disappearance of a young woman to tell the story of a community in crisis, and her gaze is both unflinching and surprisingly tender. . . . A dark but elegantly crafted book, the tension building toward a climax that promises redemption to its wayward characters."

—Holly Goddard Jones, author of
The Next Time You See Me

"Gwendolen Gross creates characters so familiar they could live next door. *When She Was Gone* reflects a perfect balance of darkness and intricate struggles, woven together with hope and redemption. . . . Some of the most powerful and beautiful language I've read in quite a while. Mix in a nail-biting plot and you have one outstanding read."

—Ann Hite, award-winning author of *Ghost on Black Mountain*

THE ORPHAN SISTER

"A trio of sisters navigates familial quirks and tragedy in Gross's emotionally charged fourth novel. . . . Gross brings abundant personality to the sisters' interactions."

—*Publishers Weekly*

"Engaging and sentence-perfect, wonderful in so many ways, but I love it best for its vibrant, emotionally complex main character Clementine. I felt so entirely with her, as she loves those around her with both devotion and complexity and as she struggles to achieve a delicate balance between belonging to others and being herself."

—*New York Times* bestselling author Marisa de los Santos

"Breathtakingly original. A haunting exploration of love, loyalty, sisters, hope, and the ties that bind us together—and make the ground tremble beneath us when they break. I loved, loved, loved this novel."

—Caroline Leavitt, *New York Times* bestselling author of *Pictures of You*

"This charming portrait of an impossibly gorgeous and gifted family is something rare: a delightful confection, filled with humor and warmth, that also probes the complex nature of identity, the vagaries of romantic and filial love, and the materialism inherent in contemporary American culture."

—Joanna Smith Rakoff, author of *A Fortunate Age*

"It's such a treat to find a great book. . . . A fun read that also has some weight to it—a perfect balance."

—*Chick Lit Is Not Dead*

"Gross presents emotional and divisive situations with a sort of objective reality that lets the story shine through. . . . The dramatic tension kept me turning page after page."

—*Five Minutes for Books*

Also by

GWENDOLEN GROSS

———

THE ORPHAN SISTER

THE OTHER MOTHER

GETTING OUT

FIELD GUIDE

WHEN SHE WAS GONE

GWENDOLEN GROSS

G

GALLERY BOOKS

NEW YORK   LONDON   TORONTO   SYDNEY   NEW DELHI

Gallery Books
A Division of Simon & Schuster, Inc.
1230 Avenue of the Americas
New York, NY 10020

First Gallery Books trade paperback edition March 2013

GALLERY BOOKS and colophon are registered trademarks of Simon & Schuster, Inc.

For information about special discounts for bulk purchases, please contact Simon & Schuster Special Sales at 1-866-506-1949 or business@simonandschuster.com

The Simon & Schuster Speakers Bureau can bring authors to your live event. For more information or to book an event contact the Simon & Schuster Speakers Bureau at 1-866-248-3049 or visit our website at www.simonspeakers.com.

Manufactured in the United States of America

10 9 8 7 6 5 4 3 2 1

Library of Congress Cataloging-in-Publication Data

Gross, Gwendolen
    When she was gone / Gwendolen Gross.—1st Gallery Books trade paperback ed.
        p. cm.
    1. Missing persons—Fiction. I. Title.
PS3557.R568W48 2012
813'.54—dc23   2012022605

ISBN 978-1-4516-8474-2
ISBN 978-1-4516-8476-6 (ebook)

TO DR. EDWARD S. GROSS, MY DAD

WHEN SHE
WAS GONE

ONE DAY

24 SYCAMORE STREET

Mr. Leonard was the last person to see seventeen-year-old Linsey Hart before she vanished into the steamy blue of a late-summer morning. He was sitting on the black-lacquered piano bench in the bay window, practicing and singing, wordlessly, along with the Schumann *Kinderscenen*. The window was open only a crack, but Mr. Leonard could still detect the wormy smell of the sidewalk as the sun struck the puddles from last night's downpour. He held his fingers over the keys to listen to the silence between songs, the breath at the end of the poem lines. Mr. Leonard loved quiet as much as he loved sound.

The night before, he'd heard her whispering into the phone, stooped on the wicker rocker on the porch, her long legs awkwardly folded, so she looked like a strange sort of beetle in the sick orange light of the streetlamp.

"I can't," she'd said. "They'd worry."

Mr. Leonard wasn't a spy; he merely had insomnia. He followed all the rules: no alcohol, walking or bicycling for exercise, warm milk, reading, but not of troublesome materials—bed for sleep only, though the book on sleep said *bed for sleep and sex,* which wasn't something Mr. Leonard worried about as a possible pollutant these days. He kept his windows open. The cicadas rubbed a brisk rhythm; even in death they were insistent, even calling out their last hope for procreation they played *presto marcato.*

"I have it," said Linsey, sweet sotto voce. "I'll bring it."

Then she went inside, her hair a long loose tail behind her, leaving him alone to wander his house, looking for clues that might help him dream.

Then it was morning. Mr. Leonard had fallen asleep in an armchair that smelled of linseed oil and Murphy's. He went to the piano, because it was always the first person he spoke to after sleep. He played the Chopin *Barcarolle* and the first movement of the Tchaikovsky no. 1 in B-flat Minor, and it was only just past five; Mr. Leonard could tell by the soft wash of the light and the hissing of dew just lit on the lawns. He started the second movement of the Tchaikovsky, then he paused.

Mr. Leonard resumed playing as Linsey stepped out onto her front porch in the hard blue light of the early morning, tucking her long hair—sandy blond, she called it, but it held mica glints, almost silver—behind her ears. She pressed against the piston slide of the screen door to prevent the usual sigh and thunk as it closed. It was five thirty in the morning. Mr. Leonard could see her without looking up. This was something people didn't know about him. There were many things, speculative and real, that people knew about Mr. Leonard. They knew he was single and aged—sixty-two, actually, though the children had simply slipped him into that category of old person, slightly scary, who gave excessive amounts of candy at Halloween and therefore was to be tolerated. They knew he lived in the house his parents had lived and died in; that his aunt had lived and died in; that a series of small dogs, shelties, usually, or West Highland whites, had lived and died in, except for the last, Moonlight. Moonlight was named after a sonata, though most neighbors thought it was just an overly romantic appellation bequeathed by a lonely old man to a runny-eyed dog who was poisoned and died in the Hopsmiths' garden. His death caused great speculation about a number of teens, but the mystery was never solved.

They knew he was a music teacher for some years at the middle school, for a single year at the high school before a combination of budget cuts and the secret of his colon cancer decided his retirement. He had the first surgery, and couldn't play for a week; never mind that eating became even less of a pleasure than it had been. But he was still alive, despite the dire suggestions of Dr. Meade, who called him personally after Mr. Leonard told the receptionist, then the nurse, then the nurse again in consecutive phone calls that he would not take radiation. He'd rather let it grow back, the way death always grew, slow consumption of the cells, whole organs, the eventual, beautiful collapse. It wasn't a fight he could win, and he didn't want the battle wounds. He rarely ever hurt unbearably, except when digesting, and that was a dull pain, a squeezing, a roughhousing of his insides. As long as he could play, as long as he had enough money and jasmine tea in the afternoons and could tote new books from the library—alternating fiction and nonfiction like an assignment—every Wednesday on his old upright bicycle with a basket. Old-lady bicycle—it had been his aunt's, his father's sister's, though she rarely rode it, so the chain had been a seizure of rust when he first wheeled it out of the shed.

Mr. Leonard had taken private piano students for some years, children whose parents evidently were not suspicious of his linty cardigans or the way he looked just sideways at almost everyone. They deposited their sleek-haired charges inside the foyer of the grand Victorian for innocuous training in culture. Then the students stopped. Mr. Leonard played his piano, sometimes early in the morning, sometimes passionately and late at night, sometimes with a languor that swept across the neighborhood like a wind-borne cloud of pollen and perfume. Once or twice, new people with money who had moved in and updated their kitchens with walk-in Sub-Zeros and ten-burner Viking stoves called the police to complain about the noise. Rachmaninoff. Brahms. Liszt was never a problem; Liszt caused children to dance on the sidewalks, or sway pleasantly in their dreams after bedtime. Generally, the police did nothing. Or they rang the doorbell and asked Mr. Leonard to please close his window, to please play *pianissimo* at least (a joke with Beau, the cop who lived around the corner on Pine. It was Beau's one "music word"—he'd been one of Mr. L.'s students in middle school), to keep it down. Mr. Leonard offered them French-press coffee. They often stopped by the following afternoon for more coffee, and sat on Mr. Leonard's wide brown front steps as if he needed protection.

Linsey knew something about Mr. Leonard, something she had shared with her boyfriend, Timmy, who was supposedly her former boyfriend since Abigail had convinced her daughter to break up with him before going to college—that since he was going to Berkeley, California, and she to Cornell they shouldn't torture themselves with distance. *You're too young to be so serious,* he'd overheard from their porch.

He'd also overheard Linsey telling Timmy this: she knew that Mr. Leonard sometimes played the piano wearing inappropriate attire. Linsey, bless her, hadn't laughed. Never mind the McGuires, two doors down, who came out to get their paper in their pj's. Never mind that sometimes Mrs. Copper nursed her baby in the backyard, and if you kneeled on the arm of one of the Adirondack chairs on the back deck, you might see her lifting her blouse for the baby's mouth—Linsey had no interest in this spying, she said, she just saw her half brother Cody in this compromising position. What Linsey knew about Mr. Leonard was that sometimes he played the piano, late at night, mind you, or so late morning might have more claim on the hour than starlight, wearing a ball gown, blue satin, tight bodice, so his pale skin spilled out over the top like added lace, or even odder: a slightly yellowed wedding dress, which Linsey assumed must have belonged to his mother.

Mr. Leonard watched Linsey pull a folded slip of paper

from the pocket of her jeans. He stopped humming—he only noticed the humming when everything else had stopped, but took comfort in knowing that Glenn Gould, too, hummed when he played; it was a kind of conversation with the piano—and he could hear Linsey sigh as she read the paper, then refolded it, then taped it to the pretentious iron mailbox her stepfather had installed on the front porch, complete with its own stubby post, and shut the door on the tail of the note.

Linsey wore a jeans jacket that was too large and too warm for August and for her slight frame. Mr. Leonard had always thought of her as a goldfinch, hollow boned, quick and certain in flight but heavy on the branches. She'd moved in next door with her family when she was three, when Mr. Leonard was still a teacher, when he'd imagined he might be *her* teacher someday, so he'd let his interest rest on her, a quiet thing. She'd always had hairdos to match her mother's then. She'd worn buns pierced with splintery chopsticks from the Golden Lee Chinese Deli restaurant her family ordered from every Saturday night. Mr. Leonard could smell their dinners through the window. They ate on the porch: moo-shu pork, orange-fried chicken, the sesame and chili oil scent floating like a casual cloud of conversation from their table to his. Mr. Leonard didn't like to sit down to eat. He liked to move, to take a bite from the carefully set plate on the kitchen counter and go get the paper. Take a bite, then empty the dishwasher, take a bite, then feed the dog, when he had one. If he didn't sit down, he didn't have to notice that he was eating, not really; he didn't have to notice that he was eating alone.

His next-door neighbors' first few years were peaceful, as the last few had been. In between, after they lost the boy, Linsey's family was loud and angry. Linsey had wept her face into angry blotches, flinging herself onto the window seat on the stairwell, which faced Mr. Leonard's house. Linsey's bedroom wasn't on that side of the house, so for him, it was as if she never slept. Mr. Leonard heard the yowling, almost catlike, territorial, of Mr. and Mrs.; he didn't see the slamming of the front door, but he saw Mr. Hart's back, huge and hunched like a bear's in a quilted winter coat, as he stalked away from the house. The ancient glass in the door, an intricate flower pattern of panes divided by wires and thin strips of wood, waited while Mr. Hart started his Volvo. But before he'd backed out, spinning tires and crushed ice over the unshoveled driveway, the glass began to fall, tuneful shards, on the wide floorboards of the porch. He saw Linsey later, picking at the bits of glass as if they held clues. He'd wanted to push open his window, call out, *careful*, but of course he didn't. She was eight, the same age Mr. Leonard had been when his family folded like a finished fan. Then her father had moved out, then the new man had moved in.

He watched the family; it was like a field gone fallow, tilled and hand hewn to remove the rocks, ready for replanting. The stepfather put in a new door, hauling the cardboard-patched broken one—thick oak and heavy—to the curb by himself on Big Trash Day. One August the twins were born,

Toby and Cody, a dark boy and a light boy, the latter bald at first, then bright blond, the kind of blond that causes casual touching; people passing in the supermarket reached toward his mother's cart, took strands between their fingertips before they knew what they were doing. Then Linsey was a teen, and she had a boyfriend. Mr. Leonard had liked him at first; he'd been one of his own students, Timmy, heavy of chest and quick to smile, chocolate brown eyes, a good laugh. He laughed a lot at lessons. He didn't practice. He had a strong ear and could plunk out melodies, finger by finger, but had no interest in picking at the tight weave of himself in search of loops of talent. That was how it worked for most people: they could find enough talent to wind together, to braid with rote skill, they could find pleasure in the music that way, even if they would never give much in performance. Pleasure in the music was something. It was like a child athlete growing into adulthood, perhaps running a little faster to catch the commuter train. The real talents—bundles and ropes of it, the kind of talent that made playing not a choice, once they found their fingers, but a requirement, even if they played passionately until college and then gave it up, always feeling the music in their fingers, in their arms, music like ghost limbs—they were rare.

He'd seen the breakup through the glass. Linsey leaning in toward Timmy, touching his face, then removing herself, fingers first, then arms, then she got up from the wicker love seat and sat on a chair by herself, wrapped only in its arms. He saw them kissing good-bye, like they always did, mouths fit together like wheel and cog, only their bodies told the rest, space between them, chests breathing independently.

Early that spring, Mr. Leonard had watched Linsey and Timmy holding hands on the porch swing like a fifties couple, courting. He'd seen the way they made their arms and legs fit together, a single body for so many limbs. He'd seen the way the love flared off them, dazzling light. Now he saw Linsey's sadness. Again. The window seat, like a crumpled child.

Mr. Leonard was a half-breed, his father a famous Jewish conductor and an agnostic, his mother a lapsed Catholic who'd died of anaphylactic shock in the picnic-blanketed audience while her husband wound his arms passionately around Mahler's no. 8 with the Tanglewood Festival orchestra. Molly Leonard had never been stung by a bee before that day, at the renowned summer festival of outdoor concerts. Perhaps it was a paper wasp, perhaps an ordinary honeybee, perhaps she had squashed it absently with her thigh or perhaps it was aggressive, rising from the earth with a mindless malice—either way, Mr. Leonard was with a nanny at the pine-beamed rental cottage. He was eight. He would swim in Long Pond, he would drink pink lemonade, hand-squeezed by the nanny, lemons and pink grapefruit, quite a lot of sugar slushing at the bottom of the striped glass; he would change into his pale blue cotton pajamas—my little maestro, his mother called him—and eat nine squares more Lindt milk chocolate than was allowed, reading *The Adventures of Tin-tin,* while his babysitter talked with her boyfriend on the phone, winding the cord around and around. He would sleep once more before he knew his mother was dead.

Mr. Leonard would've like to have talked to Linsey's mother—no longer Mrs. Hart; now she was Mrs. Stein, and she had taken a course at the reform synagogue for non-Jews who had married in and didn't want to convert, but wanted to give their homes some Jewishness (Mr. Leonard thought about this: some Jewishness, like a twig from an olive tree: like a spray can of something, eau de prewar Eastern Europe: or better yet: German Jew, crystals hung in the windows, Viennese cakes with fig fillings), so she made Shabbat dinner on Fridays. Linsey loved eating the challah; Mr. Leonard knew this because she often took hunks out to the wicker landings of the porch, fed them to Timmy, before Timmy was banished—Mr. Leonard would've like to have told Mrs. Stein not to push her daughter so hard. To let her stay with Timmy: if they were going to split up, it would happen. Linsey was young, but she wasn't stupid. Abortion was legal—for now, anyway. Children lived together now, they decided whether they fit together like puzzle pieces or whether they ought to share only meals and conversations and maybe sex but not the rest of life. The rest of life—Mr. Leonard thought—should belong to Linsey. Her mother was making the worst mistake, trying to conduct a soloist, trying to instruct her daughter's life in a way it could not be forced to go. He had always been cordial with the Harts/Steins. He brought their papers up to the porch—stacked them neatly under the rocker, bundled the mail just inside the screen door, feeling presumptuous but helpful—when they went away on vacation. They didn't ask him to do this, but he knew they appreciated it. Once, a hundred years ago when she was still a girl and he was still a teacher, Linsey had been sent over with a plate of brownies as a thank-you. She'd been eating one she had slipped out from under the cellophane as he came to the door. He heard her coming, but let her ring the bell anyway.

"For you," she'd said. "Um, for the mail."

He'd wanted to swipe the crumb from the corner of her mouth. He'd wanted to tie the lace of her pink sneaker, unlooped and dangerous.

"Thank you," he said, taking a single brownie, not the whole plate.

"No," said Linsey. "All of them."

"Okay," he said. "Except this one's for you." He removed another, just three left. The brownie tasted of cocoa, and vaguely metallic, like mix. Not unpleasing.

"Did you make them?"

Linsey was eating again. "Mmm," she said.

"Do you want milk?"

"I have to go back," she said.

"I could give you a lesson," he said, and Linsey looked puzzled, though she'd been eyeing the piano through the curved glass of the turret.

"No," she said. "I play flute. Bye." She turned and ran, and Mr. Leonard watched with trepidation, but she didn't trip. The brownies had come on a paper plate, so there was nothing to return.

Now Mr. Leonard watched Linsey leave her porch. She'd slung her little black backpack over one shoulder and she looked small under the weight of the morning light. The zipper wasn't closed all the way; he imagined the contents spilling out like food from an interrupted mouthful. She stepped out to the street as if waiting for something. Then she started down Sycamore, sneakers almost silent on the sidewalk. She walked past Mr. Leonard's house, and then she was gone.

The houses were quiet, his and hers. He fingered the keys without pressing for a while, then allowed himself a Lully minuet, softer than it should be, but innocent. It was almost nine by the time the twins slammed open the door, running for the camp bus. Mr. Leonard was playing a requiem now; he felt like something was ending. Cody and Toby kicked the screen door on the porch and let in the quick, hot breeze. A single yellow leaf fell from the dogwood in front of their house. As the boys shoved each other along toward the bus, legs long and brown, one face pinched, the other open, the note in the mailbox stirred. The breeze broke the tape's kiss with the iron, tugged the corner free from the lid. Mr. Leonard didn't see the paper as it floated free, then landed with fateful precision, the edge slipping between the floorboards of the porch. The door opened again, Mrs. Stein calling after her boys, "I love you! Have fun!" and the note fell into the lightless land between the porch's latticed-in legs and the concrete foundation of the house.

Later, when they came to question him, Mr. Leonard would try to be faithful to the morning. He remembered the note, but assumed they already knew. He remembered a lot of things, but only answered their questions. By then, the word "vanished" had wafted into his windows like the stray spittle that worked its way from rain through the screens. But vanished, Mr. Leonard thought, was a relative term. Linsey knew where she was, he thought, Linsey knew what she was seeing and hearing, what tastes touched her tongue.

He'd seen her seeing him. It wasn't as if he could help himself—it wasn't as if he was really living in his body— sometimes at the piano, sometimes inside the music. Mr. Leonard knew something about Linsey, something secret. But then, he had secrets of his own; he understood, and he wasn't telling.

26 SYCAMORE STREET

Abigail Stein listened to the hissing of the trash truck as it turned the corner from Cedar Court, the cul-de-sac. She loved that the twins were gone for the long camp day, dashed out to the bus at the curb like birds toward a handful of tossed crumbs. During the school year, they were home or on the Mom bus to sports by 2:56 PM—but camp went until four and their bus wasn't back until suppertime. Motherhood had transformed Abigail from a reasonably round object (though she was a slender woman, with softly brown, short-cropped hair, and a childlike sweetness in her rounded knees and shoulders), a red rubber ball perhaps, firm sided and elastic, into an accordion. She was always flexing out and squashing in, accommodating the music of their breath. She was always becoming smaller and larger, always folding and expanding. She turned off the coffeemaker, which still held its daily wasted half cup—her husband, Frank, wanted enough of everything, so sometimes there was too much, sometimes there was waste. Better, she thought. Better to live within his wide margins. She tipped the hot brown liquid into the garbage disposal, smelled the decay as it hit the cantaloupe rinds; she missed her husband, the boys, and Linsey.

Linsey came and went at will—she would already be at work by now with no need for a mother's breakfast or kisses good-bye. It was entirely appropriate, of course, but still startling that her once-infant could make it through days without any sort of parental support or intervention. She had named Linsey for her Scottish grandmother, Leslie, who had given Abigail a pocket-size book of fairy stories with gold paint on the edges of the pages. She didn't like the spelling with the *D*; it seemed too syllabic, too hard. Her mother wasn't fond of Leslie, her father's mother, and she hadn't wanted to hear anything about the name; she'd wanted it to be her own gift to her daughter. Soon enough, Linsey would be gone, really gone. Abigail was doing her best to let go without hysteria, but some requisite fanfare. She thought of her own departure from Highland Park, Illinois, for Wellesley—her mother's tight-faced refusal to go along for the car trip. Mrs. Cardinal hated long car trips; she'd even borne a paper bag for the fifteen-minute ride to the high school for graduation, breathing in and out while Abigail's father drove, his arm on his wife's leg, half comfort, half possession. So her mother stayed home with her laundry and alphabetical coupons, and Abigail's father and brother took her to Massachusetts, and there was hilarity along the way, ordering too much food at Waffle House (her mother insisted on cleaned plates); letting her brother, age twelve, take the steering wheel and loop eights in an empty rest area parking lot somewhere in

Pennsylvania. Roadside stands, pies they ate with their fingers. It was a wild last hurrah. Her mother never went to college, and both expected it of Abigail and never forgave her.

They would all ride together for Linsey. Her ex-husband, Joe, had wanted to take his daughter, but Linsey had asked him if he'd meet her there instead. Linsey intervened more than she should; Abigail was grateful and ashamed, as she had been all along. She knew the divorce had wrapped her daughter in grief, but she had been too lost then to peel it off, to help her enough. It was going to be awkward, the handover, the letting Linsey go to him before really letting her go. Abigail had imagined the scene, the boys playing in the stairwell of the dorm, which she could smell already, old beer and hot linoleum, and Joe would be waiting in the room like a suitor. But then he had a conference he had to go to, or perhaps it had been invented, bless him, and he said he'd just take Parents' Weekend. Which he might miss; Abigail was prepared to take over if he did.

"He won't, Abby," Frank had said, soothing her, perhaps, or riling her, she wasn't sure which. One week ago. They were in their bedroom at night; Linsey's music, Coldplay, made the walls vibrate softly.

"He might," she said. "You never know with Joe. And I don't want Linsey to expect someone and then have no one. It wouldn't be fair. The twins will have their last game that week, the regionals. In Ramsey. Will you go if I have to go to Cornell?" She planned ahead. Not for everything, but for the things that worried her the most.

"I'll go even if you don't."

"You're managing me," she said, squeezing his broad back as he sat on the bed, his legs crossed ankle to knee to untie his pretty brown lace-ups. Abigail had been suspicious, at first, of her second husband's vast collection of Italian shoes.

"Maybe," he had said, leaning back against her. She loved that he was so big. She loved feeling small beside him, a bird in a lion's paw.

Now it was almost time, just another week left before they took her daughter away. Abigail walked up the steps, listening to the music from next door, Mr. Leonard, playing Chopin, or maybe it was Beethoven, very fast, insistent, a bit wild. She liked Mr. Leonard though she didn't have much to say to him. She was afraid he'd heard every argument through the windows, afraid he might mind them as neighbors, and at the same time, she resented his early morning playing sometimes, or late night, even if it was spectacular, it wasn't always what she wanted, it wasn't her particular brand of passion and grief.

Abigail smoothed her short linen dress. She checked her makeup in the mirror—the first makeup she'd worn in days, and it wasn't for the women's group at the temple, where she felt welcome and shunned at the same time. It wasn't for Frank, a lunch date; it wasn't for coffee with any of her friends in town—most of them were still away in Long Beach Island or Cape Cod. She had dressed up for Margaret, her Wellesley roommate, who was now a management consultant—a partner, in fact—with a company that owned its own glass-and-chrome dagger of a building in midtown. Margaret had an office the size of Abigail's living room. Childless, single, she was the target of the "me finger" diamond advertisements in the *New York Times Magazine*.

Abigail's cell phone rang as she was locking the door.

"Resumé?" said Margaret. "I should've had you e-mail it, but you remembered, right?"

Abigail chuckled. She did have a resumé, folded in halves and quarters and wedged into her Coach bag, her one purse, between her tiny new spiral notebook and her long checkbook wallet, which she always thought should have MATERNAL stamped on the cover.

"I'm serious," said Margaret. "Just because you're not talking full-time yet doesn't mean it has to be Gap or Starbucks. You can do better, lady. This is your apprenticeship, your chance to decide what's next on the Grand Abigail Itinerary."

"I'm not even sure—," started Abigail.

"No," said Margaret. "You called me, and you know how I am. You're sure. I'm excited. Morgan Library at noon. We're so ladies who lunch, you know; no one here has lunch before two."

"Okay," said Abigail, because acquiescing was what you did with Margaret. When they were roommates, Margaret made everything a hunt, a battle, be it dates or choosing the best dining hall or graduate school, where she went immediately after graduation. Harvard. Abigail had married Joe, and had relinquished her casual dreams of art school, or art history, or maybe trying B school herself—though that was just Margaret's rabid influence. Abigail had never really wanted to fight that fight. Or any fight, really.

After the divorce, Abigail had worked at a nonprofit arts agency for three years, administering grants. There were things she loved about work: the purposefulness, the sense of spreading pleasure to children and teachers, giving them a dance troupe performance, a puppeteer for a workshop; she also loved dressing up for work, flirting in the elevator, going out for lunch. She'd met Frank at a benefit. And four months into her twins pregnancy, she'd given up the job, thinking it wouldn't be for good. She still thought that when the twins were one, two. By the time they were three she knew she couldn't juggle like that; she'd have to wait and start with something else, something that let her check in at nine and check out at three. Still, she'd always daydreamed about having an arts café—art shows hung monthly on the walls; music performances and poetry readings coupled with divine desserts, chocolate-raspberry cakes and espresso with perfect *crema* in thick cottage blue cups.

Margaret indulged Abigail's dreams. "When you open your café," was something only Margaret said, regularly. She wanted to help; she wanted to see Abigail doing, the way she had when Abigail was lost and needed to emerge from her darkness. It was Margaret who forwarded her the job opening after the divorce, Margaret who lent her a suit for her first interview.

They met every four or five months for lunch in the city, though Abigail realized she'd let it go too long this time—over a year. Last time a school nurse had called her home because Cody had broken his collarbone diving for a kickball.

Margaret still made everything a project, and was ruthless in approach, whether it was trip planning, a nanny quest, or buying a new black dress. She helped Abigail with all her acquisitions and battles—and flushed with the pleasure of the endeavor. When Abigail had needed a divorce lawyer, Margaret had met her in Hoboken, a first, with a vanilla legal-size folder, a box of tissues, and a baseball cap with MAKE ME spelled out in rhinestones on the crown.

"This is for going incognito," she'd said. "When you want to dress up as someone other than Supernice Abigail and stop thinking about everyone else and make a list of wedding silver, dining sets, bank accounts, testicles, whatever you really want to get from the bastard."

The train was full for midmorning. Abigail squeezed into the middle seat and recognized a man across the aisle—Charlie Sentry, her neighbor. She'd always assumed he was off at the crack of dawn, and back after bedtime, because she'd never seen him out retrieving the paper from the walkway or seeing off the kids. She'd made quite a few assumptions about him, actually, as she had many of her neighbors, perhaps because they seemed so uninterested in her, and she'd never questioned the shield of invisibility from house to house, even when they could hear each other's voices from sidewalk to open windows.

He wore a suit, but he was surreptitiously eating an apricot Danish, and she worried for his white shirt. It was kind of charming, eating forbidden food on the train, and his eyes were open wide with childlike pleasure. Then he tucked the paper bag into a briefcase and started chatting with his seatmate, a woman in a long, soft dress who laughed and leaned back, revealing a strangely long neck. She reminded Abigail of an otter.

How did people do this every day, commute? How did they spend the whole morning getting from here to there and then plug themselves into there, producing work like the electricity that ran their empty houses, refrigerators and airconditioning chilling and lights lighting and clocks counting the minutes of absence? Was this what she wanted to do—work in the city, or even work in town? She had spent too much time living in her house, too much time using its walls like her own skin.

She transferred in Secaucus, and her neighbor disappeared. She walked off the train in midtown, feeling the heat from the sidewalks and buildings, a whole summer's worth of heat. She saw a young woman with hair like Linsey's disappear around the corner and almost stepped off the curb before the light changed. An arm reached out to stop her—it was Margaret, early for once.

"You're early!" she yelped.

"Ready to become a working girl?"

"Probably not," said Abigail, but Margaret waved the thought away as they crossed in the stream of pedestrians, and walked up the stone steps to their lunch destination. Then she was folded into her friend's wings, where she spent an hour and a half eating chicken salad, looking at the correspondence exhibit at the library, noting all her possibilities, and letting herself be the pure subject of Margaret's marvelous passion and attention.

6½ SYCAMORE STREET

It was nothing like *The Graduate*. First of all, she wasn't that old; her oldest was in high school and Jordan was done with college, practically a man, though practically, she thought, not actually, despite how he made her feel; he still had this particular hesitance, this asking for permission, that occasionally made her cringe when they were together. But he did know what he was doing; there was nothing virginal about the way he pushed her up against the door inside his diminutive carriage house, the way he liked to keep their clothes on, to thrust past unzipped teeth and the crotch of her underwear pulled aside. There was no way around the fact that he thrilled her, that she thought about him when she was emptying the dishwasher and came without touching herself, that his mouth was just the right amount of hard and narrow, that he was rough enough, but never cavalier. Second, it was nothing like *The Graduate* because, despite his underlying indecision, he had come after her. Fully.

One morning she'd been at Starbucks with Helena, ordering her usual—a single shot of espresso with hot water and a tiny dollop of foam, which she and her friends called short-hot-shot; it was their joke, only she said it a bit too loudly at the bar, waiting for her drink, and the barista, a young man who looked familiar, as if he was one of Steve's friends; perhaps she'd seen him in the local paper as captain of the hockey team, said, "Short hot shot for you, gorgeous." He was young, but deeply masculine, his mouth lush and ironic, his black hair glossy as wet stone. It was as if they were in a bar, a real bar, a drinks bar with desperate men and flashy ones, with women who were hot without trying and women who were trying too hard. She hadn't been trying anything. She was a housewife. She talked mostly to women, to Helena, the Group, to children and to cashiers and on the phone to mail-order folks in Wisconsin who joked about the kids' footie pajamas with comforting aplomb and thanked her for being such a good customer. She was; she was a good customer. But she'd forgotten how sexual she had once been, until this young man.

"You're not short," he said, handing over her drink. He didn't collect her money—he tapped the cup and his lips, mouthing *gratis.*

It made the back of her neck warm, the movement of his mouth, the implication. Her blood diverted the course of its circulation, determined new necessary spots, prepared itself for animal intentions. It was absurd. He teased her one day, another, and then she started going for coffee at least daily. He was a kid and she was sucking down designer drinks and giving herself reflux by leaving out the half gallon of milk she ought to use to soothe the lining of her esophagus.

Whitening her coffee with milk reminded Reeva of her great-aunt Bertie, who was always complaining about her gas and reflux and saying things like, "Oh, I can't possibly have that, it'll make me fluff," the worst moniker for farting Reeva had ever heard, to this day. Bertie was pigeon breasted and let her hair go gray, then dyed it so it shined a glossy light blue. Bertie was prone to streaks of jokes, which made her laugh so hard Reeva suspected it had made her wet herself. Reeva feared she might become like Bertie, but crass without the joy. She had this postpartum problem herself, and always had to wear little panty liners. She kept a Post-it with a *K* written in red permanent marker on the dashboard of the Explorer, but she hardly ever remembered to do her kegel exercises anyway, and if she ran more than a few yards, if she laughed too hard, she peed just a little. It was horrifying.

The thing with Jordan had started eight weeks ago, when Charlie was going to Utah twice a month for some project that bored her so much she didn't listen when he told her about it and then she felt guilty when she had to ask about his day in great abstraction. She worried, a low-grade, chronic worry, that maybe Charlie had found someone else. She was sure she was turning old too young, not listening, wetting herself. Pathetic. Then one day she was looking in her closet, digging out the short leather skirt she got between Tina and Johnny, when she'd been using the gym religiously, every day, for six months, and had a flat enough belly to buy herself something new and sexy. Charlie didn't really like the skirt, made his special silent grimace of disapproval when he saw it, but she wore it to Starbucks and, just as she'd imagined, only better, Jordan had said something about it.

"Nice skirt," he said, leaning over the counter, putting his long-fingered, hairless hand too close to hers. His skin looked so smooth, she thought, too young.

"I thought I might get something for my friend," she improvised, waving toward the overpriced coffeemakers. "Can you help me pick something out?"

"Mmm-hmm," he'd said. What was she doing? It was Starbucks, and asking for help was respectable enough, even flirting was respectable. Charlie probably did it at work all the time. She knew Charlie's office, the glass walls, the heating always up too high, the women who bronzed their naked legs and sported Jimmy Choo shoes, much too much sex for a tax attorney's office. She'd flirt if she were he.

Jordan had been very disrespectful, helping his suburban housewife customer with the coffeemakers. He'd led her to one, then another, first brushing her arm, then leaning against her back as he pointed, explained, whispering about the steamer and the dual spouts and the built-in grinders. He spoke too close to her skin; his voice burned her. He'd taken her to the back, holding her hand—right there in Starbucks, gripping it as if they were supposed to be partners on a field trip—to look for more stock, something that might be on sale, and he'd turned her, his hand on her shoulder, to look at some boxes, then he'd run his other hand right down her ass to the bottom of her skirt, and he'd touched her thigh, just gently, as if her skin was firm and fragile as an egg. He'd spun her in like a dancer to face him and he'd kissed her hard; his mouth tasted of too-strong mints and of dark-roast coffee.

"Jesus," she said.

"Jesus good or Jesus bad?" he asked. "I'm never sure, since I'm a Jew."

She'd laughed. She'd had no idea he was a Jew. In her fantasies, he'd played rugby. Like her husband. Like Charlie. It was pathetic, her fantasies were pathetic, and her behavior was pathetic.

"Jesus good," she'd said, anyway. "And Jesus bad. You do know I'm a grown-up, right?"

"Um, so am I," he said, standing straight. Such a boy, his mouth pursed. "I should tell you I have a little problem."

"Jesus," she said again. She was thinking that this was a cliché. She was a cliché. Middle-aged housewife pretending to be young again. Affairs, they were a cliché. She didn't believe in them. She loved her husband. Her kids didn't deserve this. But then, she did. She deserved the intense desire she felt, that she wanted to grip his thigh between hers, Jewish or not, twenty-something or not. Wasn't this the kid who skipped a year of middle school, some genius kid or something? Really good at the piano? She wished she could remember all her local history. She could almost conjure up a picture in the local paper—she had noticed it when it was in her living room: an almost entirely symmetrical face, like a trick, which half is which, only a tiny beauty mark, a small dark pen dot on his left cheekbone, to differentiate the smooth landscapes. She kissed him back. He slid his hands up into her skirt, but she stopped him short of reaching into her underwear. Not because she didn't want him to, but because of the panty liner. Pathetic. Exquisite. He had a wonderful mouth.

"About that problem," he said. His face was bright, two circles of pink on his cheeks. A boy doll. Incredible long lashes. No red in his scleras, such new, coffee brown eyes. Even the brown wasn't worn away from the overbrightness of days.

"Fine," she said, listening to her own voice, as if she were a character in a play. "Tell me, ruin the moment."

"I have a problem stopping. I don't want to stop," he said. He was reaching up inside her shirt now, his thumb on her nipple. She moaned. She didn't mean to. She realized clichés existed for a reason. Other people did this. It was a comfort, knowing this bad behavior wasn't original. It felt so good.

"It's just that sometimes my body kind of takes over and I can become inadvertently aggressive," now he was pinching her. It was ridiculous, shocks of heat in her crotch. "So you need to really tell me if I *must* stop."

She would learn later what this meant. It meant sex with the boy was exhilarating, like almost drowning, like falling, like climbing trees as a girl, unsure of the footing but sure of the direction—higher. Her body had forgotten all this modulation, all this raw sensation. It meant sometimes she tried to get him to slow down, and that excited him, and that his wiry arms were strong and he might pin her down. That she liked that, too, despite herself. They selected a code word, "cellophane," which meant she really wanted him to stop. She floated inside it, the miraculous bubble of desire and satisfaction.

Between physical bouts—gorging themselves—Reeva did learn some things about Jordan. He wasn't really Jewish, just his father was, and even his inherited surname wasn't identifiable, House. Plain and strange. Perhaps it had once been Hausenstein or something, Jordan speculated. He liked to claim Jewishness, the intellectual identity, and it fit him well, though Reeva hadn't seen inside his particular kind of lust for argument, for knowing, in anyone else before.

He ate like a child out of control. He told her how he drank coffee all day long at his job, filling and refilling one giant paper cup per day—he didn't want to use more than one because it was wasteful, all those cups in landfills taking ages to biodegrade, but he liked the taste better in paper than in a mug. He didn't like mugs; the texture of ceramics bothered him.

On his breaks Jordan walked over to Kings and bought half a dozen Krispie Kreme doughnuts, which were his food all day. She was tempted to bring him some of her famous pork stew, but she didn't want to mother him. He had a mother, Elizabeth, to whom he referred by her first name. He had a photo of her as a young woman in a prom dress, turned so she looked over her shoulder at the camera. There was something imperious in her glamour, and she looked like him, long lines, long fingers, secret eyes. Now Elizabeth had multiple sclerosis and walked with a cane. She was living with Jordan's aunt, her sister-in-law, in a big house in Fair Lawn now—Jordan's childhood home had netted enough money for his college, for his graduate school if he ever went, for his sister's medical school at Yale, for his father's new habit of betting on horses when he wasn't working at his veterinary practice in Yonkers, where he grew up. He was semi-retired and Jordan said he still hoped Jordan would go to vet school or at least medical school someday.

At least medical school made Reeva chuckle. No one was parenting Jordan now, though, and the way he lived reminded Reeva of her sons, made her imagine what horrible habits they'd relish if she were indisposed. Sometimes he ate a four-pack of iced walnut brownies for dinner. Two prewrapped cheese sandwiches from the little Italian market on Hope Street. No lettuce or tomato. Mustard packets squeezed directly into his mouth. She had never seen him eat anything green.

That first week she brought him a bagel sandwich, beautiful pastrami, which she hadn't eaten herself in years, let alone bagels, so densely caloric, and he picked at the edges, eating the sesame seeds. When she pressed him, he told her he didn't like meat of any kind, and he abhorred mayonnaise. *Abhorred.* Sometimes, after they finished and she was getting dressed, he grabbed the notebook at the side of his bed and wrote. He was left-handed. The crook of his arm, to keep the ink from smudging, moved her—poor lefty, different. The veins on his skin so thick and close to the surface, the same blood that filled his penis.

Sometimes he wrote equations, or musical notation, sometimes he wrote in Latin; he refused to tell her what it was about. "Nothing," he said. "I have nothing important or original to say, yet I feel compelled to express myself, so I just write it down and let it go."

She knew it must be brilliant. He made these bizarre connections, between the distance between leaves on the maple tree that leaned over the carriage house and the spaces within a crystalline structure like a snowflake. He knew about the cut and flaws and color of diamonds—lord knew how and why—and he told her all about her own, the one she wore on her engagement ring, the three teardrops on the anniversary necklace that sat just a little too low between her breasts. He pressed his finger into the center one until it pricked and bled.

He was the smartest man she knew. Boy, not man. She realized that intelligence wasn't just the body of knowledge— he had that, he knew all about classical music, murmuring, "Trout Quintet," when her car radio played it, murmuring, "That's too aggressive, it's supposed to be adagio." He knew about the wines she brought him, Charlie's wines, client gifts or pleasure purchases. Jordan lay the bottles on their sides between the books he had more of than anything else in his messy little nest. It was a fire hazard, really, his carriage house full of books and papers and a cello lying in the corner of the room like a corpse. It was cello he'd played, a prodigy. He'd played with the Julliard Orchestra as a seven-year-old; he'd won competitions and played solo at Carnegie Hall at eleven.

He gave it up before college, he said, waving at it, dismissive. But it was still with him, the tawny animal of an instrument, out of its case, on its side like an odalisque.

"Play for me," she said, feeling brave. It was a heavy summer day and the carriage house smelled like rot and sugar. Charlie was at the office; Steve was at his camp job; Tina was still at a sleepover; and when Johnny came home from camp, Linsey Hart, the sweet girl from down the street, would come meet him and babysit. One more week and her best babysitter was off to college. She hated losing confidence that way, confidence, and invisible time like this, with this boy, in his hovel.

"I don't play it anymore," he said, looking away. He pulled his hand from her thigh. Her body cooled a few degrees—modulating. She loved his hand on her thigh; she was confident of her thighs because she had been regular, all these years, about aerobic and then water workouts and now yoga and Pilates at the New York Sports Club, where she watched her friends drop out, one by one, replaced by younger and older, but not forties, not her age, when it was crucial you keep moving or risk permanent sag.

"Why not?"

"Because," he said.

"Why not?" She was teasing, but she wanted to know. She wasn't in love with this boy, she told herself, she couldn't be, but she wanted to eat his history, suck him up, be a girlfriend. Pathetic, she thought.

"Tell me," she said, her voice harsher than she'd expected.

"Fine," he said, looking away from her. "I played it for Emma Gold senior year. I was in love with Emma Gold. She was incredible; she had this exquisite long hair. Not quite red—not brown. She was superior, but she earned it. Until high school I thought she was a snob, but she was just busy *doing,* while I was busy *thinking.* Wasteful. Mental masturbation."

As he spoke, Reeva saw herself for who she was, practically middle aged, no girl with long hair, the hair Jordan was lifting invisibly in the air. High school wasn't that far away for him. She'd worn bell-bottoms in high school, and in the cycle of fashion, they were back again, a sure sign she was ancient.

"She went to Oberlin," he said. "She was going to be an ethnobiologist, or do genetic research. And on the *side,*" he said this with contempt, "on the *side* she was a better musician than I ever was. She sang, this huge voice in a long lean girl. Sang like Ella, *and* sang like La Divina—" He looked sideways at Reeva. "Maria Callas, of course." And Reeva hadn't known, but she had heard of Maria Callas. Maria Callas was for her parents' generation, not this kid's.

"She ran track and had these long legs." Jordan was lapsing into lazy language. Jordan didn't speak like this. She must have been incredible, Emma Gold.

"And she quit the singing, and she got her degree in fucking *English.*" What was wrong with English? Reeva wondered.

"And she married some guy who took her to make hammocks on a commune in Canada. MARRIED." He spat it out. "She's fucking twenty-one years old."

Twenty-one, Reeva thought. I sure hope that's younger than you. But she didn't ask. She tugged the recalcitrant shade over the window. Last week she'd been straddling Jordan on his bed, his hands on her breasts, when she'd looked out the window and had seen her son and Linsey Hart walking through the woods. Johnny rode Linsey piggyback. She'd grabbed her own clothes and ducked down to close the shade, but stopped and looked, kneeling on the floor. The dappled light through the maples mottled their skin. Linsey had a pink team sweatshirt from the high school tied around her waist. Johnny wore a blue T-shirt from Steve's elementary school soccer team—he didn't play. Pink and blue. Girl and boy. They matched, a set, youth and youth, in a way she'd never match with Jordan. In fact, Linsey was a better match for Jordan. Reeva was expired milk, she was finished. Johnny started to slip, and Linsey hitched him up, higher on her back. Reeva had been clutching the windowpane, absent from the room, absent from everything but her son's weight on a young woman's back, and she thought maybe Linsey looked up. Maybe Linsey saw her. Maybe Linsey had seen the Acura on the street, two houses down to be discreet. She'd told the girl she was going to a meeting for Library Friends—she'd even checked to be sure there was a meeting, but it wasn't on this street, it was at the Library Café, and here she was, her face visible to someone who might walk past on the woods path, naked in the carriage house rented by the college graduate between commencement and purpose.

Today she wouldn't be accidentally exposed.

"More," said Reeva, ducking away from the window. She touched the symmetries of his face, long perfect nose, the corners of his mouth that held judgment and private pleasure. "I want more," and as usual, Jordan was happy to oblige, pushing her down onto her knees on the bed, not gently, exactly, but with a kind of comforting purpose.

3 CEDAR COURT

Though he was less than a year older than the twins, and catty-corner behind them on the cul-de-sac, their properties kissing at the edge like the tiniest overlapping of universes, George Amos Whitebread didn't play with Cody and Toby. It wasn't that he eschewed boys a few months younger than he was, or that he was a loner by nature, or that he wasn't often outside. In fact, Geo was always outside, measuring the depth of the snow in winter with a wooden yardstick he found in the basement, caking pinecones with peanut butter and rolling them in birdseed in February, chipping away with his fingernails at the pitch-sticky bark at the base of the almost dead white pine in the corner of his backyard.

He had gone to church summer camp for two weeks, though at ten he was already agnostic, and considered the prayer session and Bible stories they told, sitting in a circle on the floor of the youth room that smelled of dust and Juicy Fruit gum, to be propaganda. His mother wasn't particularly religious, and the story was that his father had quit the church when they married and were supposed to go to counseling for a week beforehand. He didn't like the priest's breath, he said, burnt onions. Geo's parents told him things, spoke in front of him about sex and politics and about his own strange situation, as if by not addressing him directly, they were not exposing him to the strange workings of the adult world. Geo liked it; he felt respected. Basically, his father was a skeptic and his mother was angry with God, but the church camp was almost free, and all three of his sisters with their windy long hair and crackly white voices had gone, so Geo went, too. Then he spent the rest of the summer in his room or in the yard or at the little local lake, where he played for a lethargic hour or two on the raft with the boys his age, feeling the sun soaking into his skin, the water repelled by his natural oils. Then he moved on to the deep end, answering the guards over and over, who should recognize him by now, *yes,* he was a member of the club, here was his badge, and *yes,* he had passed the deep-water test. Sometimes he said *yes, sir,* even to women, but the irony was lost on them.

"Geo!" his mother called from inside the house. He knew he didn't have to go in until the third or fourth warning. He was unearthing a small colony of pill bugs from beneath an early-yellow sycamore leaf. He touched them and they curled.

"Because of Megan's Law," said his next-door neighbor, the twins' mother, as she opened the car door. He could hear everything on their driveway, the pieces of conversation that left their beginnings and ends inside the doors of house or car.

"No," said her husband, Mr. Stein—Mrs. Stein had her phone on speaker. "Just no." He had a smile Geo liked. And his voice was deep, the kind of deep that made your own breastbone vibrate.

Mr. Stein had come to speak at career day at school last year, and afterward, while everyone was standing in line for the school-lunch oatmeal cookies Geo didn't like—too dusty—he'd come up to Geo as if Geo was a real neighbor, the kind who came in and out of the back door without knocking, one who shared in screaming for business at the lemonade stand.

"Howdy, neighbor," Mr. Stein had said. "I didn't know you were in the same class as Cody."

"And Toby's last year," said Geo. Toby was actually a decent kid.

"And Toby's. Last year. I guess I should know your name. Mine's Frank." He grinned. He almost seemed nervous.

"Geo. For George. Or the earth. I kind of like that better."

"You aren't as shy as they say," said Mr. Stein.

And Geo, because he liked his neighbor's voice, because he knew his own voice would be wide and deep someday, said, "No, I'm not actually shy at all."

He knew he was different, and most of the time he didn't mind, but in summer he was tired of being taken for a visitor from some Paterson youth group, or some lucky kid from the Fresh Air Fund. He *was* some lucky kid, but not the way they thought he was. They thought he was some lucky kid because he'd been rescued from what was rightfully his—poverty, drug addiction, all the horrors of not having. Actually, he was some lucky kid because his sisters were relatively cool, and now that Caroline was off at NYU, living in the city year-round, he had his own room, and he had only two chores: emptying the dishwasher and keeping his gerbil, Clive, clean, fed, and alive. He was lucky because he had everything he needed and many things he didn't, because his mother had finally made a name for herself hand-making silk and cotton baby sweaters for boutiques in town and on the Upper West Side.

Ever since he could grapple, Geo loved sorting things that looked similar and different. He used Merry's camera, downloading photos by the time he was six, sorting, arranging. He was the king of the kitchen cabinets, making the spices alphabetical. For his ninth birthday, his parents bought him a used Nikon camera he'd coveted from the camera shop in town. Its silvery body was an empty notebook awaiting possible poetry. He saved his allowance for film and prints from the drugstore in town, where they knew him as one of their last regulars at the photo counter. He cut and glued collages onto oak tag or poster board or abandoned scraps of wood, creating order out of the chaos of photo after photo, mining individual faces from groups, faces in backgrounds, faces in mirrors. He crafted collages of his mother, one of each of his sisters, Caroline, Merry, and Victoria, using the old shots he'd scanned in from baby albums and current pictures. He used corkboard he found at yard sales, constructed popsicle-stick-fence frames. He constructed a collage of his neighbor Toby, who appeared in the background of shots he took at Westfallen Park, where the dog run made a great shooting ground, or simply hidden in the corner of a series of shots he took of the corner of the main street and his cul-de-sac, showing the year's procession of recycling bins, used Christmas trees, green grass and dun.

Geo made a collage of Mr. Leonard the music guy, who appeared in shots he took at the arts fest in town, the winter carnival when the horse-drawn carriage clopped along Broad Street and people sat and noticed the storefronts instead of scurrying from one to another. People's faces were different around animals.

Trimming the photos revealed people Geo might not have otherwise seen—Tina Sentry's mother, her face turned upward in one background, looking at someone out of the picture. In another Mrs. Sentry held a look of fury, standing behind the fence at a baseball game—the expression was so intense Geo discarded the scrap, but it recurred in other shots. His collages were like his mosaics, about sameness and difference. Deeply right and satisfying, like filling a necessary well with sweet water.

Just last week Geo had had enough photos of Toby's big sister, Linsey, who was going off to college, to make a collage. He'd trimmed and pasted, shellacked the finished board and let it dry, only he felt embarrassed at the thought of offering it to the family—he'd have to talk to the parents; he'd have to commit to their front door. Plus, in some of the pictures, though he'd trimmed around his face, Linsey was kissing her ex-boyfriend, so she looked contorted, almost desperate for air. He'd save the collage in his desk, where ungifted expressions waited.

For his father, his sister, his art teacher Mrs. Greenberg—with whom he shared a disdain of still lifes—he offered as gifts their collages or family collages or neighborhood collages on thick paper.

Despite being born a bit of a mystery, baby Geo had grown up in the ordinary fashion, learning letters first and then numbers. Learning the workings of his body. It wasn't until he was four years old that he had noticed. It was as if he'd been unaware of his separateness until then, that the cautious teachers who included Kwanzaa songs and paid special attention to Martin Luther King Junior Day at his preschool hadn't gotten to him. It was his best friend, Minal, whose long-lashed oak brown eyes watched everything the way Geo's did, taking in, taking in, storing and classifying—they were best friends from the first day of preschool, when Minal had announced that she would be sitting with Geo from now on and Geo made no protest—had asked him, "Geo, you know you are black?"

"I am a boy," said Geo, because this was generally the main distinguishing feature in preschool. Brown eyes or blue or green, hair color, boy or girl. Minal used to joke that she was a boy, too, but he'd never claimed to be of the fairer sex.

Fairer. Minal had skin almost as dark as his, and long, licorice black hair. She also had a little dandruff and two other girls teased her, saying she had lice.

"No," said Minal. "You are a black boy. I know because I am an Indian girl."

"One little, two little, three little Indians," sang Geo. He didn't sing with the group, but he sang with Minal. The two of them were in a corner of the sandbox, their corner. The other children were knocking over a sand castle in the other corner or stepping on ants under the slide.

"Not that kind of Indian," instructed Minal.

"What kind of Indian?"

"Indian from India. The way you are black from Africa."

"I'm not from Africa," said Geo. "I'm from Ridgewood."

Only that night he looked in the mirror over the bathroom sink. He stood on his toes on a stepstool and watched his face for long enough to really notice, then inspected his mother, his sisters. His mother knew what he was doing as soon as he took her hand and rested it, palm down, on the table, then rested his beside hers.

"Am I black from Africa?" he asked her. "The way Minal is Indian from India?"

His mother sighed. She put his hand inside hers, a small warm stone, though he already didn't like to be held as closely as he used to.

"You are black," she said. "Your skin is dark. But you are black from white," she said. "Because Mommy and Daddy have light skin, but they have some dark skin in their genes.

We made *you*; you are ours, no matter what anyone else says. And probably the dark-skin genes are from Africa."

"But I'm not from Africa," he said. "I'm from Ridgewood. Are you from Africa?"

"Part of me must be," said his mother. "Because you are from me."

When his neighbors were coming or going, Geo was tempted to lean over the fence, to say something. He was always tempted to join in the music of their conversations, but it was just pieces, and he didn't belong. Their door sighed closed.

He had a collection of items that he kept in the fence gap: wine bottles from his parents' recycling bins, or others out on the street every other Wednesday, with their Spanish and French labels, bright graphics or subdued woodcuts, their hard grape scent; he liked how they moaned different notes when he blew across their open tops. For a while he kept bricks he found, pieces and wholes, in the woods just up from the pebbly stream bank. There was a place people dumped things—beer cans; cigarette butts; blue plastic *New York Times* baggies of dog poo; the ends of construction projects, like the broken bricks and dregs of cement and occasionally paint cans. He thought of it as a graveyard, these abandoned projects, and he picked up bricks for a while, carefully avoiding the squish of the blue bags as he stepped into the site.

But his mother had found the wine bottles and took him inside and sat him down to talk about alcohol. Geo had tasted beer and wine at his parents' table and once at Merry's secret party when his parents went camping by themselves for an overnight at Bear Mountain and she was in charge of him, but he didn't particularly like either the taste or the dizzy feeling he got after having too much at that party. So when his mother was worried about the wine bottles, it was hard for Geo not to laugh at her. He didn't, though; he told her he didn't drink but he'd stop collecting. Then he had moved on to the brick bits, last summer, until someone, and he suspected Cody Stein, had knocked over the wall he'd been building, a dry wall, which meant there was nothing between his bricks, no mortar to hold them together. So it could've been the wind, or it could've been Cody, who had been peering over the wall all that week, bored because he was home sick from soccer camp with hoof-and-mouth disease. He had sores on his lips and Geo had pretended not to look at him, not to see him looking, because he knew Cody didn't actually want to play with him—he'd learned that years ago when he went to play once at Mrs. Stein's insistence, and Cody had taken Geo's Pez dispenser, called him a fag, told him he'd have a turn with the stomp rocket that never came, and spat at his own brother, Toby.

No wonder Geo didn't play with the twins. And "fag" wasn't the only name Cody called him, and Toby, too, even if he didn't shout it out the way his brother did. Marshmallow. Oreo. Booger.

"Can you talk at *all*?" Cody teased when he said very little. Maybe all the names weren't for his blackness, maybe they were for his shyness, but they were still mean. Especially Cody. Toby was quiet the way he was, and once he came over to look at Geo's bottle caps. But they weren't going to be friends, it was a matter of distance, of those two fences, of the way his mother called out of the back door and the twins' mother or a babysitter was always with them, watching.

He was working on his bottle caps this summer. He collected them down by the river in the woods and in the alley behind the ShopRite, picking them out from cigarette butts and crushed plastic bottles sticky with artificial sugar. He had collected the wine bottles with Minal, before she moved to St. Louis. He sometimes went to dial her phone number in Ridgewood before he remembered she was gone.

The bees loved the caps. They visited them like flowers. Geo arranged his findings in the silky dirt between the fences, the Steins' fence and his family's. Two fences. He knew the Robert Frost poem, and wondered whether two good fences made them the best of neighbors, or canceled out like a double negative.

He had a Yoo-hoo, a Tusker lager, a dozen Cokes, and two dozen Diet Cokes, pressed into the soil, flat on top like coins. Occasionally the beer caps had dents from bottle openers, but mostly they were twist offs, and had to be eased in so they wouldn't bend. Eagle Rock. Stewart's root beer, cranky Red Dog, swoopy Orangina, Snapple after Snapple, Zima, round-edged Fruitopia. At home they drank two-percent milk ("What's the other ninety-eight percent?" joked Merry. "Air?") and Victoria's favorite, orange juice, and when she was home, his oldest sister, Caroline, drank bottle after bottle of vitaminwater. She was getting too thin; Geo knew it from her face, her hair looked almost gray it was bleached so pale. His newest Caroline photo collage showed the change.

The wind blew hard, dusting him with piney soil. Sometimes trash collected in the spot between the fences. Sometimes Geo found Cody Stein's homework or the prescription label for Tina Sentry's acne medication.

Today, there were some new papers in the crease where the fences narrowed into an oblique angle, and Geo rescued them. A bill from the milk truck that delivered to the Sentrys' house where there was always a gaggle of kids and the mother wore a leather blazer and swore sometimes in front of them. A water-stained scrap of box from a frozen shrimp Creole entrée. A note, folded and folded again, wet so the ink bled through the white side of the paper, so the thin blue printed lines had swelled into the spaces between them.

"Mom" he read. He peeled it open and examined both sides, but "New" and "L" were all he could make out. He refolded and tucked this into his pocket. Geo wadded the other trash in his hand as he made his way to the cans behind the garage.

"THIRD TIME, GEO," his mother called out from the back door.

"Can I have a soda?" Geo asked, because he was bored. He already knew the answer, and she didn't even bother.

"Wash your hands," she said. "Cookies? I want you to help me tie on some beads."

26 SYCAMORE STREET

She was home by three, still abuzz from Margaret's inexorable enthusiasm and three iced tea refills. Maybe she wanted to open a *gift* shop, she thought, fingering the things she loved on the shelf in the hallway, the tiny cloisonné boxes, the carved wooden birds from a roadside stand in Vermont, which had sold rabbit meat, eggs, maple syrup, and the glorious little painted birds: a chubby robin, a slightly haughty red-winged blackbird. She had been with Joe when she bought them.

Or maybe a restaurant. A tea shop. The women of this town would like that, a proper English tea. Margaret always stretched the frame of her world; Margaret always reminded her of the possibilities still there for the grasping. There was a business proposal course at the community college—none of this was too hard for her, it was just the sum of it that seemed daunting. For now, they'd agreed, she'd try out something part-time—to eavesdrop on the small business world, to wind the gears of something before trying to make it tick.

The bus would be back soon from camp, and Linsey would get a ride home from someone at work; the empty house would be full. She went upstairs and changed back into jeans. Passing in the hall, she sniffed; the boys' room felt stuffy, so she opened the windows, airing out the crushed-grass, sour sweat as best she could, waving her hand, ineffectual. She looked in their drawers, always embarrassed to be prying, but she needed to keep them safe from their own curiosities. She found pennies; gum wrappers; a thousand tiny plastic party favors—superhero wobbly heads, ball-and-cup games; hardened, unwrapped licorice; collector's cards with their peculiar Japanese characters; a picture in Toby's drawer of the basketball team Toby had quit while Cody kept at it. Nothing dangerous. She still regretted not paying more attention to Linsey's drawers when it mattered, to Linsey's teenage hiding places. Leaning her face against the screen, she could almost smell September out there, the leaves letting go of green.

Since it was summer, Frank would come home early. He came home early as often as possible. He played catch with the boys in the backyard. Connect 4 with Toby, over and over, at the dining room table. He took Linsey shopping for the things she needed that Abigail had not managed to find for her, or with her. He mixed piña coladas and planter's punches for her, and sometimes for Linsey, and brought them out to the yard, where mother and daughter sat with their feet in an old tin tub that used to hold Linsey's vast collection of Beanie Babies before she donated them to the day care in Paterson where she now worked. The school was in a warehouse in a horrible neighborhood with a gun shop two doors down and loitering lost men on the street, but Linsey and her coworkers traveled with buddies and pepper spray. She could give the kids attention they wouldn't otherwise receive. She was there right now, but her mother was already ahead, thinking about the evening, swatting the invisible mosquitoes, wondering whether they had any bendy straws for the boys' virgin version of the punch.

Never mind the phone, she thought, as it rang. *Let it ring,* she had to put away the three baskets of laundry waiting on the landing. *Let it ring, let it ring,* and then she dashed across the landing to the master bedroom to answer it anyway, because Abigail had a hard time ever letting the phone ring.

"Is Linsey Hart there?" asked a young voice, a bright bird sound. Maybe it was the new roommate again. Linsey had talked with her for two hours just last week. They had texted and talked on Facebook relentlessly. Preparation for friendship.

"No," said Abigail. "She's at work. May I ask who's calling?"

"Oh," said the voice. Chipmunk, really, but sweet. Very young, maybe someone from high school. "No, I mean, this is the day care—I didn't realize she had two jobs. It's just, we thought she might come in today to pick up her last check. But we can mail it to her."

A squirrel, that strange squirrel bark.

"No," said Abigail, confusion rising in her, almost like nausea, pressing her breastbone, making her dizzy. "No, she's there today, isn't she? I mean, she's working for the rest of the week?"

"Um? Maybe you should talk with her? I mean, who is this?"

"Her mother," said Abigail, feeling strong suddenly, feeling stern. This silly rodent of a girl had clearly not been outside that little office at the front of the ugly industrial building today. She clearly didn't know anything about Linsey.

"Oh, I thought so," said the girl. "She decided not to work this week—isn't she going to college tomorrow or something?"

Now Abigail wasn't only confused and stern, she was also unsure what she was supposed to say. So she simply said, "I know."

"Right, then, so can you give us the address at college? I mean, so we can send her her last check?"

Abigail recited the address. It was visible as a card in her memory, the box number already assigned. Just yesterday, she'd sent a little postcard there, one with a picture of the town square, so Linsey would have a tiny bit of home with her when she arrived, so the box would have something waiting for her. She liked to have things waiting for Linsey. She still left notes in her clothes sometimes, little love notes in the pockets, the way she'd written tiny poems on the lunch bags Linsey carried to elementary school, small enough so only Linsey really noticed, light blue pencil or even yellow, Linsey's favorite color. Her little girl, her sunshine.

If Linsey was not at work, where was she? Sometimes she babysat for Reeva, down the street, but it wasn't on the calendar. Abigail walked into her daughter's room, knocking first, though the door wasn't latched. She half-expected a sleeping form in the bed, a woman's body curved around a teddy bear. Her daughter's scent was in there, lilacs, crushed green, sassafras, milk. The bed wasn't made, the teddy bear hung on to the edge as if he'd been climbing down on his own. The trunk was in the corner, almost filled: the extra-long sheets; the pillow; a new laptop; the new nylon underwear buried among the cotton Abigail had bought for her, forgetting her daughter was now private about underwear; a framed family portrait with Frank and the boys (Abigail had already found the old portrait, with Joe and Linsey and herself, pregnant, though she hadn't known it, with the lost boy, slid between the cardboard backing and the front photo. She'd been surprised by how tender it made her feel, mostly toward Joe, Joe before they each lost a necessary piece); and on top, two new sweaters, the lilac cashmere one Frank had spent way too much on as a surprise, and the old moss-colored wool one that used to belong to Joe, which Linsey appropriated and wore when she went out on the weekends, never when she went to visit her father—there was always a chance he'd ask for it back. It was vintage 1950s, and still held the vague odor of his clove cigarettes and occasional pipe. Abigail was afraid to go near it.

She dialed the Sentrys' number—maybe Linsey was babysitting—but got the answering machine. Reeva Sentry made her uncomfortable—she fit into the neighborhood in all the ways Abigail did not. Her Christmas lights went up at Thanksgiving. She had window boxes themed for Halloween and Easter.

Abigail tried Linsey's cell phone, but voice mail picked up right away. "Call me, baby, okay?" she whispered, trying not to sound wretched.

Afraid. That was it—she was afraid now. She was afraid because she didn't know what she was supposed to do. She knew what it was like to lose yourself in panic. She remembered the night her son died, her first son, the one she'd lost at two weeks' old when Linsey was only five—she was still bleeding from birth, her breasts were enormous and painful. Her baby hadn't cried out to be fed and she'd slept six straight hours. She woke because of the heat and weight of her milk, her uterus throbbing, the floorboards smooth and cold as Popsicles, the light of early winter morning gray and gentle, and she'd stumbled into his room, mumbling, *good baby, what a sleeper, thank you, baby, for the sleep, but now you need to nurse.* She'd been the one to find him and she'd been the one to call an ambulance, knowing it was far too late; she'd been the one who had to express her useless milk in the shower, who'd made milk for a year and a half after he was gone, her body still hopeful. She'd been the one who'd mourned so deeply she lost herself, who'd left her little girl alone in the world, who'd fallen into her bed and stayed there for almost eleven months, unable to leave, unable to walk farther than the bathroom, unable to bear her husband's hands—too rough, too old, his voice too deep and his eyes too reddened—unable in all the ways of the world.

She'd come back to them, but too late for Joe. Not too late for Linsey, who seemed to forgive her daily, all along, who brought her little projects—bouquets of dried flowers, acorns glued in collages with dandelion leaves and milkweed seeds—into her mother's sickroom. She sat on the square of sun by the closet and worked quietly. She kissed her mother's hair, not her face, as if she knew such direct sweetness was intolerable. Abigail's mother had come. She hadn't kept the details, but she remembered the fear that stayed with her all those months, the fear of looking up, the fear of what she might find, though she'd already made the worst possible discovery. And soon after she recovered, the fighting started. And soon after the fighting, the long division of divorce.

Abigail wandered down the stairs, trying to be casual about it all. If it doesn't know you're afraid, it might not attack. She stood by the phone, tracing numbers on the cacophonous sheet taped up to the wall. More than half the numbers were Linsey's friends. She dialed the ex-boyfriend's parents, hanging up without leaving a message. They were awkward with her since the breakup. Or before. They were people who served milk in tall glasses at supper and used cloth napkins. She tried Timmy. It was for the best. She'd wanted her daughter to have a pure first year of college; she'd wanted her not to make things bigger than they were simply because of distance. She'd wanted safety.

There were dozens of scratched-out names, dozens of friendship dead ends. She tried Bethany's cell number, but she got a message, a recording of some loud music, then giggling, no polite instructions whatsoever. They were still so young. She called Markos, who had had a crush on her daughter since the third grade, and whom Linsey had tortured with chaste friendship. Maybe. There were things Abigail didn't know about her daughter. She'd learned this last year with the drugs. She'd found the pot and the single tab of acid in Linsey's room in a little wooden box Abigail had brought her from the honeymoon in Greece. Olive wood, with monkeys carved on the lid, it had a gorgeous smell all its own. She'd wanted to put Linsey in rehab right away, she'd overreacted, she was so scared of losing someone else, but they'd gone to counseling instead. Linsey said she'd only used pot twice; she hadn't even tried the acid. Abigail had decided to believe her.

"Hey," said Markos. "You ready?"

"Excuse me," said Abigail. "It's Linsey's mother, not Linsey." She wasn't used to caller ID protocol, even though they had it, too—she always said hello and allowed the caller to announce herself, even if she'd read the name on her phone.

"Oh, Mrs. Hart," said Markos, because he still didn't remember. She didn't correct him, *Stein*. "You having a party for Linsey or something? She thought you might—" And that hurt, because she hadn't even thought about it, she'd been wrapped up in planning Frank's vacation time and the boys' soccer camp and the days they needed to drive Linsey to drop her off. She hadn't been that generous. She hadn't thought enough about how her daughter felt.

"No, I mean, that's a nice idea. But I was just wondering whether she's, um, hanging out with you today? She was going to be at work—at least, I thought—" She swallowed twice. She was not going to give him the whole story. She just needed him to tell her where her daughter was.

"Mrs. Hart? Oh, well, I thought Linsey wasn't leaving for a few days? I have until September seventh, can you believe it? Columbia starts way late—and it's not like we have far to drive or anything." She'd forgotten he was going to Columbia, she'd thought it was Yale. She was glad it wasn't Yale—she liked Markos and thought Yale was too self-important for him. Then, she was a little worried about her daughter at Cornell. So big, anonymous. She'd leaned toward a small, liberal arts college herself, Oberlin, or Grinnell, Wesleyan, or Antioch. She'd liked the warmth of those places, the safe feeling they gave her on their college tour, junior year.

"So she's not with you?"

"No, man, I wish she was. I have no idea what stuff to pack. I have so much stuff." There was something plaintive in this. "Will you tell her to call me anyway when she gets back? I tried her cell yesterday but her mailbox was full or something."

"Fine," said Abigail. She hung up. Her gut hurt. She wretched slightly and stood over the sink, waiting. She called Linsey's phone again. Voice mail. Then she dialed her husband's number, because Frank would know what to do.

444 SYCAMORE STREET

Timmy was running. He had hated the running workouts for crew, grudgingly pounding the stadium steps and flocking through the neighborhoods with his whole team, like starlings, but now he needed to burn. If he sweated enough, if he hurt enough, he might shed the cells that touched her, he might be able to soften the pain enough to stop its screaming.

He had loved Linsey Hart since fourth grade, since she told him the pointillism project he'd labored to make wasn't the epic failure he thought. Mrs. Greenberg the art teacher had sighed and told him it was interesting, but even at age nine Timmy knew "interesting" was a doubtful proposition.

When they finally kissed, just two years ago, it was very different from the kisses of ordinary girls. It was far from perfect—they'd caused the horrible music of tooth on tooth, and then when he went in for a second attempt he'd accidentally bitten her lip, but it was the kind of love worth working for. Now they were experts at kissing, and not just kissing—she was the first girl he'd slept with, and he wasn't sure he ever needed to sleep with another; his body missed her body the way another body might miss water when parched.

Timmy was packed for college. His mother wasn't at all nervous, not like Linsey's mother, who had pried them apart like halves of a walnut for nut meat. It was wrong. Just because *Abigail* had made a mistake marrying her college sweetheart and grown bitter at the loss of her own possibilities didn't mean Linsey and Timmy couldn't grow together, even by being apart. He'd thought about waiting to enroll at Berkeley—even though he'd applied early and already had his uncle Geoffrey, a gallery owner in San Francisco, arrange for a coveted tiny share apartment in an old Victorian in Berkeley just three blocks from campus—he'd thought it was a mistake to leave her. They hadn't had sex until two weeks before Abigail made her proclamation, and once they had, he couldn't have enough. She couldn't, either. There was nothing old-fashioned about it, and it was far more than anything the music or the TV or the movies or the videos promised—it was better, and it hurt to want something so much. They'd skipped almost a week's worth of classes, coming back to his house after homeroom to tear at each other with need, or to gently explore everything about this way they made something no one else had ever invented.

His chest burned with breathing. Timmy nodded as Mr. Leonard the music teacher passed on his bike, his basket filled with library books and a neatly folded paper bag.

He'd be Tim when he got to Berkeley. He was weary of his diminutive by the time he was ten years old—only four foot six, but bored of being Timmy, the *y* like a tag of infantilism. His dad was Tim, though, and he couldn't have the same name as his dad, even though they'd named him that way. Timmy went to sleep-away camp that summer he was ten, and told everyone he was Timothy, though half the time he didn't remember to respond to calls across the pond or the music tent and people thought he was aloof. He'd made a best friend, James, and they'd spent all free periods in the cabin, discussing video games that were verboten at camp, the junk foods they missed. Then one afternoon James had laughed too hard at Timmy's joke, and had leaned in toward Timmy's mouth with his own, crushing him lip to lip. Timmy screamed, embarrassed, a little girl's scream, and left the cabin. He'd always felt it was his fault, the ruined friendship, the fault of the Timothy appellation. But in California he would be Tim, never mind his father. If his uncle called him Timmy it could be pleasant nostalgia. Timmy had grown up a while ago, even before he'd finally had his mouth on Linsey's smooth skin. It was going to be freedom to let his name match—one hard and simple syllable.

Timmy had packed one suitcase and one backpack. His flight was booked and his parents were already in California, stopping to approve the apartment and visit Uncle Geoffrey for a few days before going to a Peace Corps reunion in Rarotonga. The house was already on the market. They'd spent years at home because of him—he knew they thought of it this way even if they never said it—and now they could go back to being expatriates, to being helper people, to being *away.*

He never realized before how many women of his town

were runners. Jogging strollers passed him as mothers he'd seen under baseball caps in the stands pushed past, faces hard, fully inside themselves. Who had kids in high school and kids in diapers? In this town, the women folded around their children like envelopes around letters. His mother was disdainful—not that she didn't care, but she didn't think her whole life should be getting him from one place to another, only to be ripped and cast off when he was delivered into adulthood.

Dr. Sill ran by in the other direction on Maple, his arms pumping. He'd been Timmy's elementary school principal, a sweet-faced man with caterpillar eyebrows and a great grin who stood outside the school waving as parents dropped off their charges. Timmy had read in the local paper that now that he was retired, Dr. Sill was writing children's books.

Everyone did something. Everyone had a spot. Timmy belonged inside Linsey, beside Linsey, linked to Linsey. If he could leave, maybe he'd have back the half of his arms that belonged to her.

Before he and Linsey had sex—and as much as he loved her before, the glue of being together the way they'd been made it impossible to separate, too painful, too much tearing—he'd always wanted his own *away,* and Berkeley was away without having no family anywhere. Besides Linsey, there'd be nothing left in this town for him. If Linsey ever came back to this town. If Linsey followed orders.

He passed the last of the little Italian delis on the corner of Spring and Ivy. In middle school they'd gone there in packs for slushies after the last bell. Linsey would be there with her friends getting Ring Pops and making her mouth scarlet with sucking.

He had been running every day this week, his last week. He ran halfway down her block, peeking over the fence at that kid Geo's mosaic—bottle caps and glass. Geo had taken pictures of them together—the kid was always out with his ancient camera, and at first it had seemed innocent enough but recently it made Timmy nervous—his every action potentially arrested. Geo was odd, but Timmy was sure he was brilliant, poor thing, some sort of genetic trick played on him so his parents, natural parents, were white, while he was black. In Berkeley, Timmy thought, no one would blink. In this town, people were very small about difference, about seeking otherness.

Sometimes he ran at night and went past her house and looked to see if she was in the window. The last time they'd been together on purpose she had worried the whole time about whether they might be found out. They met in the woods by the boulder kids painted with initials every year; theirs had been on twice but now were buried by new lusts and pairings. The woods smelled of old oak leaves, of the musky tannic river, and of beer. They'd had sex, Linsey pressed up against Timmy on the rock, then he'd pushed her down into the leaves. They'd both worried about ticks afterward; she'd worried about being found out—it wasn't good, for the first time. Since they'd been together, he'd learned to taste her joys like lemon and coconut; her sadnesses were metallic, stale. She'd tasted of sorrow that last time, and he'd let her walk back up the hill to her house alone. He'd almost wished someone else would meet her on the way, someone else would take her from him, someone else might even hurt her, so he didn't have to do the hurting all alone.

DAY TWO

36 SYCAMORE STREET

With the window open, the kitchen smelled of summer: the cedar deck was wet, and waves of odor lifted from it in bands as the sun struck. Unkind sun, Reeva thought, late-summer sun, never reaching the mildew under the boards, but scorching her hanging plants between the dousings of storms. Green rot.

"I told you I don't want toast," muttered Tina, Reeva's fourteen-year-old daughter. "I only eat fruit for breakfast." She rummaged in the fridge, then opened a granola bar and ate it standing over the sink. Reeva resisted the urge to smooth Tina's cowlick.

"I need money," mumbled Steve, opening Reeva's purse.

"Steve," said Reeva, without moving toward him. "It isn't polite to dig in my purse without asking."

"I asked," Steve said, but he kissed her cheek before leaving the room. At sixteen, he knew the power of a kiss.

She loved them too much as she watched them leave for camp. Steve collected his backpack, cheese sticks, soda sneaked from the basement party storage; both older kids wore earbuds and iPods, insulating their ears from her ordi-

— 71 —

nary kitchen. Tina was there but just barely, scoffing at the toast Reeva still made for her, butter and seedless raspberry jam. Her youngest, her imperfect, beautiful Johnny, seven years old, was making a sculpture out of twist ties from bread bags, humming to himself and leaving the bread to stale.

"Johnny? You want breakfast?"

He didn't look up.

"Baby? Breakfast?" She rubbed his shoulder gently. Tina snorted.

"It's a garbage truck!" announced Johnny. Reeva felt herself clenching everything: jaw, biceps, hands, thighs, prepared for Tina to say something noxious about her brother.

"Eat your breakfast, please?" She kissed the top of his head, which smelled of cinnamon.

Johnny stuffed the corner of his toast into his twist-tie morass.

"Eat, please," said Reeva, hating the hardness in her own voice. Johnny sighed and pinched a tiny piece of bread off the slice. He smacked his lips as he ate.

"He ate, Mom, you happy?" At least Tina didn't attack him.

"I ate," said Johnny, grinning at his sister.

Then they were gone, and Reeva felt their absence in her chest, a crushing sensation, her lungs constricted for potential pleasures and slights.

The house hummed with machines: the fridge, the basement dehumidifier, the new brushed-steel dishwasher, which she shut with her hip—last night, as usual, her husband,

Charlie, added his wineglass and didn't reseal it, so it didn't run and when she shut the window, switching on the central air, the kitchen stank of sour milk and onions from the stroganoff. She blamed Charlie. She loved Charlie, but maybe not enough to accept this habit of his of making everything just a little more annoying. The coffee grinds he spilled on the counter. The paper filter sogging halfway out of the garbage barrel, spilling its stain and drip onto her white tile floor. Charlie had been against white tile, but Reeva knew it brightened the room. She was still selling houses two years ago when they renovated the kitchen; she still had a visual library in her head of what worked, what brought rooms together so the houses looked like families, living and family and dining rooms holding hands, and what made them look like mistakes. Bright yellow kitchens, blue-flowered wallpaper, ceilings painted dark red—mistakes. Clean counters and floors, walls in Benjamin Moore's classic whites, which really offered a drop of ocean, a pinch of woods, really not just white, or wallpapers that didn't suck you in but expanded the space: small flowers, gentle tones; these were what made you want to buy and move in today.

Reeva had an hour before the Group would be over. It was Tuesday, and she wished she'd asked her house cleaner to come on Monday instead of Wednesday so she wouldn't have the lint of ordinary days to contend with before she had to contend with the women. She'd been thrown from her easy horse of order when Linsey had failed to show up to babysit for Johnny after camp yesterday—she'd come home from

Jordan's hovel just a few minutes late, but Johnny was sitting on the back step crying, locked out of his own house, because Linsey hadn't met him there. Linsey had been so reliable; Reeva thought, for just a second, that she'd screwed up the schedule herself, but once they were inside and Johnny had a tall stack of apology Oreos, Reeva checked the calendar. It had been Linsey's fault, and she didn't ever answer her cell when Reeva called her for an explanation. Reeva didn't have the parents' number handy—they weren't the type of neighbors whose number graced her bulletin board. She'd just suffered her small fury and moved on.

Now here were Charlie's leavings. The kids' thousand plates. Only three kids, but they used twelve place settings for the few bites they consumed before their clattering departures.

She wasn't really in the mood. Never mind that she started the Group to begin with—just as she had started the Five back in high school. Her select few. Never mind that the weekly meetings kept her from changing the wallpaper in her own living room once a month now—like that postpartum-maddened woman in *The Yellow Wallpaper*—now that she didn't have work to keep her distracted. Johnny didn't need her as much as he used to. He was seven, and though he still had ADD, would always have ADD, he was getting by in camp, and in school. He had an IEP now, a plan to help him through the meltdowns and the times he sat at his desk lining up the bits of paper he'd torn from the edge of the holes on his notebook. No medication: Charlie had wanted to try it, so they'd tried it, and it made Johnny's mouth dry, kept him up at night, caused him to gain six pounds—though it was supposed to impede appetite. He didn't need that, to be chubby as well as distracted. He had always been beautiful: pale gold hair, when her other children were brown haired. Green eyes, the kind with the golden center and rusty flecks in the irises. She'd loved him as a baby, perhaps more than her others, not that she played favorites, but Johnny had been hard to soothe, he'd needed her so much; she'd despaired of ever not carrying him in the snuggly, and then he was three, and then because the teachers had hinted he had something wrong with him, she was taking him out of the extended-day preschool all her children had attended. Then the gym class where he was the only one who wouldn't come to circle. The two-hour Montessori class was too much independence; he dumped paint on the rug squares when all the other children carried their Dixie cups and brushes with care. They didn't disparage him there, but they did suggest that at four he might not be ready for preschool. Then specialists, then a diagnosis. The drugs when he was five. One month later she took him off, not really consulting with Charlie; not really caring if he cared.

Reeva met with the school social worker once a month or so. Things were under control. They didn't even know at camp, hadn't *needed* to know, which she considered a coup. The neighbors didn't know; her mother-in-law didn't know. Her sister knew, but her sister had breast cancer, which had murdered their mother, so she was deep into her own battle and didn't help or hurt much for knowing. The Group didn't know. She'd thought about telling them, but it felt like giving away a part of Johnny, her golden boy.

By the time the women rang her doorbell and came in, not waiting for Reeva to open the screen door for them, more comfortable in her house then their own (or at least that was her intention), Reeva had vacuumed, put brownies none of them would more than nibble in the oven (except maybe Christine, who was getting a little rounder than her usual plump size fourteen these days), emptied the dishwasher, set out cups and half-and-half in a pitcher and pink and blue packets in a bowl, and dusted invisible cobwebs from the mantel and the windows. She'd noticed the margins of dust behind the couches and made a note to tell the cleaning lady to be sure to clean there. She was a wonderful Brazilian woman, but she was a bit bossy—easier to instruct by note than in person. When Reeva was working, she had someone come in twice a week, but now once was enough. She never got the panes on the built-ins in the dining room clear enough to suit, no one ever did except Reeva. Charlie called her obsessive-compulsive. It used to be a loving joke.

The women started talking about the time the sewer main burst and the street was closed for a week. The men had parked the cars on Lake and they'd all trudged on the snowy sidewalks holding their noses and cursing the neighbors who shoveled thin pathways instead of investing in snow blowers.

"And Beth's car got sideswiped," said Christine.

"You know," said Reeva, handing out mugs, wishing it

wasn't too early to drink wine. "I don't think Beth Boris lived here then."

The women sat around her new kitchen table, admiring the newly landscaped backyard—the weeping cherry with its tag still festive around the narrow trunk, the spindly, hopeful forsythias—and accepted their mugs. The "I Love Mommy" mug Tina made when she was five went to Helena; Two Mexican daisy mugs from Reeva's honeymoon for Andrea and Mazie, who were about equal in her affections; the slightly-too-heavy mug with the cracked copper glaze that had appeared in their house, too beguiling to toss, too mysterious to like, about a month ago, to Christine. It hadn't just appeared, in fact, this mug: she'd somehow acquired it from Jordan, strange and desirable, living in that little carriage house behind the Hopsmiths' until he decided what he wanted to do with his college degree. It seemed so bizarre from this angle, her body with his.

"Oh no," said Christine. "Beth did, she's been here longer than any of us."

Reeva didn't like it when the women tried to tell her neighborhood history. Especially about people like Beth. They'd had a little falling-out, Beth and Reeva, so she would prefer not to hear about her neighbor with the pool except when said pool was clogged with tannic oak leaves, or when her toilets backed up. Not that she was vindictive, not really. She looked at the half-and-half she'd set out for her friends, but didn't pour any. Black coffee gave her a horrible acid stomach, but she couldn't afford to gain right now.

"No," said Reeva, "I don't think so. Beth moved in after us." But now she was going to be gracious and let it go. This was the weekly meeting of the Group. They were meant to be working out schedules for playdates, the very lax and unofficial babysitting co-op; they were discussing the teacher assignments for the fall again—something that bored Reeva at this point, having sent three through already.

"I can't believe they haven't replaced Mr. Leonard with a full-time music teacher," said Helena. Helena played the harp in a professional orchestra. She performed at the Episcopal church and had her own recitals in a series in Upper Saddle River. Reeva always went, though she didn't love harp music. She did enjoy watching her friend transformed from the straggly ectomorphic mother of three, who looked like she fed them all her food and went hungry, into an angel in a halo of hair, a pale, almost colorless blond. She wore soft makeup that made her eyes dramatically cerulean.

"I can't believe they're giving Jordan Miss Elephant. I just finished her with Chuck," said Christine.

Reeva had started when she said Jordan, though Christine's Jordan was a common topic. She'd been anxious lately. About Jordan, about Charlie, about the mugs and the landscaping. She missed checking the new multiple listings. She shouldn't have retired.

"She's not so bad, Miss Elephant*en*," said Helena, kindly.

Even if there were teachers she liked more than other teachers, Reeva wasn't the kind of mother to put up a fuss—not anymore, anyway. When Steve had been in first grade, he had the vindictive Mr. Peterson—the man had simply mistaken Steve's shyness for reticence or rudeness. A few meetings with the principal had straightened that out, at least enough. They were all happy when June came, but at least Mr. Peterson had stopped giving Steve completely inappropriate detentions, and Steve had never lost his place on the football select league for absence after school.

"No," said Andrea to Mazie, privately. They were a little too quiet, talking together and not for everyone, but Reeva let it go.

Mazie looked up. "This woman I called to sit Janey?" she explained, caught out. "I told her I couldn't pay eighteen an hour for a sitter. Twenty an hour for a cleaner is fair, after all, toilets and everything, but sitters don't have that much to do. Especially at night."

"Who do you use now?" Mazie turned to Reeva. Reeva sighed. She was tired of this conversation, too. "Cleaner or sitter?"

"Or dentist!" Christine was slightly hysterical. "I'm looking for a new one. Dr. Needleman—I should have known just from the name! He didn't match my color very well with this veneer." She bared her teeth. Reeva was *this close* with Christine. Ever since Christine had asked her for Linsey Hart's number, and then booked Linsey for the dinner they were both going to at Indian Trails Club for the Cancer Research Society—calling her as soon as she opened the invitation. It was morally reprehensible. Friends don't steal friends' babysitters. Christine had had a live-in for six years and she'd just let her go, since her boys were eight and ten now, and Christine wasn't *really* working. She was an agent, too. Sold mostly condos, so they'd never really been competition. Christine looked annoying in her little white BMW, too small for anything except work—her enormous boys, and Reeva meant enormous, Christine should've stopped trying to feed them so much once they passed the one-hundred-pound mark; they couldn't fit in the little jump seat at the back of the Beemer.

"Actually, I use Dr. Needleman," said Reeva. "I gave you his name."

"I'm happy with Schwartz, in town," muttered Helena, but with a sweetness that allowed Reeva to forgive her.

"Oh, I heard he had an affair," said Christine.

"Why would he do that?" Helena looked up from her cup. She glanced at Reeva; they were in collusion for less than a second. "His wife works in the office, doesn't she?"

"Accounting," said Reeva.

"It just isn't right," said Christine, tapping her teeth, then opening her mouth for everyone. She looked slightly feral. "Don't you just hate making your kids brush? I know we're supposed to, but don't you all just let them get away without sometimes?" She looked around the table. This is where the women were supposed to say *oh, I know.* This is where they were supposed to open the arms of normalcy to make Christine feel less alone in her oversight, in her negligent parenting.

"God, no," pronounced Reeva, relishing the *no.*

"That's really not fair to them, is it?" said Helena. Reeva knew she was on her team.

Andrea and Mazie looked nervous, as if they'd just witnessed a hit-and-run. The old lady was down. Should they come to her rescue, or call 911, or just pretend they hadn't seen and let someone else cope with the blood, the broken drugstore sunglasses?

"And considering their diet—my God, no brushing . . . ," said Reeva, going in for the kill. "You wouldn't want them toothless by twenty, now would you?"

Mazie laughed nervously. She looked at the clock—an antique, Charlie's mother's bequeathal. Too tinny, the tick. Christine went orange under her makeup. Reeva never trusted her color, always wondered about tanning booths. The self-tanners were enough, even if they faded fast. No one used tanning booths now—such an indulgence. And skin cancer. She thought of her sister and softened for a second.

"I have to go," said Mazie. "Sorry. Allergist."

"Me, too," said Andrea. She didn't get up, though. She sipped her coffee again. Reeva made delicious coffee.

"I know a dietician for children," Helena said to Christine, and Reeva adored her.

"Never mind," said Christine. She was getting up. She hadn't said why she had to leave, which was the Group's convention.

Suddenly all the women were leaving, except Helena, who was clearly going to stay for the deconstruction after they'd gone. At the door, holding her purse like a weapon, Christine turned to them, Helena and Reeva, the new team.

"Did you hear about Linsey Hart?" she asked. She'd saved something. It was going to be the big coup at the end of the meeting, when everyone was leaving for lack of conversations. She had planned to be important, Reeva could see.

"She was supposed to sit yesterday—I can hardly ever book her, and then she didn't even show up, or call," Reeva said. She couldn't let that go.

"No, I mean, she's disappeared."

"What?" Helena leaned in. She did the unthinkable; she wiped a crumb off Christine's shoulder, an act of forgiveness.

"Might have run away. It's only been one day, but I heard from Beth Boris at the Whole Foods that the police came and everything."

Beth Boris, Reeva thought, I should've known. They had probably *planned* to meet up at the Whole Foods. Then it hit her—*disappeared*. Her chest suffered with the effort of breath. Linsey didn't show here—or anywhere. This was not a girl who would run away, though honestly, Reeva didn't know much about her family, just that she was hard to book as a sitter, just that she had been reliable and then failed to show. This didn't happen to teenage girls in this town—they got in trouble for smoking pot, or they had sex too young, or they crashed Mommy's Prius, but they didn't disappear. All the dangerous possibilities closed in on her as the group digested this idea and fiddled with their key chains. Rape, murder, kidnapping—beautiful Linsey Hart, whom Steve had secretly loved since he hit puberty. She knew by the way he swiveled in the backseat of the car when they passed her on her bike, her long hair like a flag, waving under her helmet. She wore a helmet, Linsey—she wouldn't get in a car with a strange man. She was going to some good college, wasn't she? She never overcharged for babysitting.

Perhaps her mother wasn't particularly neighborly, but little-girl Linsey had come to the door at Halloween: a cat, a puppy dog, a bird—always an animal. She'd opened her own door for Reeva's kids as she grew older—handing out three mini Snickers, a whole handful of M&M's packets, generous with chocolate and grins.

What do we know of any of our neighbors? Reeva wondered, as she stood in her doorway, seeing off the Group. She imagined Linsey Hart, who was beautiful, who was young, who had parked out in front of Reeva's house sometimes in her boyfriend's little car and kissed and kissed as if there were no windows on Reeva's house. For a second, her heart hurt for Linsey's mother, a tiny, loud woman she didn't particularly like. Divorced. Remarried to a Jewish man, remade herself a bit, as if being Jewish could be acquired. Someone she would never have invited to the Group, but still. She stuffed awful ideas back in their box—the girl was about to leave for college; that time made kids vulnerable and brash, a final senior skip. Probably Linsey had just gone overnight to friends. Her heart closed again. But she forgave Christine, just the tiniest bit. It was big news, after all; she'd be watching for that tiny car in front of her house, she'd think about it until the girl came home. Or was found. Which had to be soon. She shivered, refusing to allow thoughts of search dogs and bones.

Reeva felt a special connection to Linsey, not only because she was patient when she babysat, not only because she saw Linsey taking Johnny for a nature walk through the woods that afternoon when Linsey was babysitting and Reeva was looking out the window of the carriage house at 6½ Sycamore and maybe, just maybe, the young woman had seen her through the glass. Reeva wasn't sure whether she should hire her more or less after that; she went for more. Linsey wasn't the kind of girl to get into trouble, and even if she did know more about Reeva than Reeva might like, she was an excellent babysitter. Responsible. Safe as houses, she thought. Safer, probably, than her own Tina. She wondered about her own girl for a minute, off at high school, more concerned with her friends than anything in her home. Reeva went back inside and shut the door.

The detective had just looked like a policeman to Toby, a policeman with a big head and a sweaty pink nose, and no square plastic hat. He loved the plastic hats; last year he'd been a policeman for Halloween and his brother had been some stupid Mortal Kombat character *again*, even though you were supposed to be someone different every Halloween, and Toby wore a great hat, square and shiny with a thick blue fabric, from a collection of costumes Dad had bought them when they were really little, like four or something.

She'd been gone only since yesterday, though since she was under eighteen, just barely, a single day was long enough to "start the process," as the detective said. Mom wouldn't explain anything, except to tell them Linsey would be home soon, about which Toby wasn't entirely convinced. His chest hurt, like when he had asthma. It didn't prevent him from breathing, just from ever feeling full of breath.

This afternoon after camp Toby wished his father would have just stayed home. Mom was pulling out strands of hair, something she hadn't done since the drug thing with Linsey. She was making them a snack, oatmeal cookies from slices of premade dough that tasted way better raw, all oat and butter. One by one she rested them on the tray, as if they were each very important. She'd forgotten to preheat the oven. His mom slid a forefinger and thumb to her scalp, tugged, then pulled out a single dark brown hair. She looked at it and did it again. Toby watched from the family room floor, where he was picking old stickers off the cover of a Kumon phonics workbook.

"Hey," said Cody, letting the back door slam as he came in. The grass smell came in with him, and the air conditioner hummed into action.

"If Linsey never comes back, can I have her room?"

Toby watched his mother. It was as if she was letting it take her slowly, like a disease. She pulled out another hair. She glanced at it, then let it drop, horribly, on the cookie sheet. Then she pushed the sheet gently across the counter, and it slid onto the floor. The circles of dough stayed put, but Mom walked out of the room, up the stairs, shutting her bedroom door behind her.

"Stupid," said Toby.

"You're stupid," said Cody, trying to grab the book from him.

Toby pulled it to his chest. He thought about following his mother, but he didn't want to see her face now. "You really want your own room?" he asked.

"Nah," said Cody, but Toby knew he did, he really did, even though it was Cody who made annoying smacking noises in his sleep, and Toby who let his brother leave the light on when he preferred the smooth texture of darkness.

Toby was really worried about Linsey. Of course Mom was worried, but Mom worried about everything, about finishing homework and that it was right, about dinner being hot enough, about when it wouldn't be shorts weather anymore, about the mole on his earlobe—she'd taken him to Dr. Burger, who had frozen it and cut it off right in the office, which was sick, and the mole was just a mole after all that, not one cell of cancer.

He had gone into Linsey's room a lot since she'd disappeared. He wasn't supposed to, of course, but he'd been doing it as long as he could remember. He used to go with Cody before Cody got bigger than him and kind of rude. Of course he loved his brother. Of course his brother was like him in strange ways; they had the same way of holding pens and pencils that wasn't wrong enough for the teachers to complain, but wasn't quite right, either. Their fingers were always stained, thumbs dented. Neither of them liked tomatoes, even though their parents did. They still had some words in their secret language that no one else knew, though Cody had told Banks, the big-headed doofus on the football team who was Cody's kind of best friend, about one word, "Speakey," which was just the word to mean their language, so it wasn't that secret, but still.

When they were really little, they used to go into Linsey's room all three together when she babysat. She didn't mind them all of a sudden, when she was in charge. They huddled on her lavender-scented bed under the pink-and-blue lily-dotted comforter—the strange country of a girl. They took

Linsey's funny ladybug flashlight into their impromptu tent, and she told them stories, weird stories, not ghost stories exactly, but stories that meandered around and had bad parts and good parts and lots of candy and discovery but no endings. She had stories about visiting the moon, about finding apartment buildings there with elevators—because Toby liked elevators. Linsey gave them tiny candy bars from the stash she kept in her drawer (until one time when Cody went in by himself and ate some and left a wrapper on her bed, because Cody didn't think things through all that well), and they sang the songs they liked the most and also one hundred bottles of beer on the wall, which was funny, because Linsey said one hundred bottles of milk, or one hundred bottles of Yoo-hoo. They'd both loved her then, but Toby loved her more.

When he went in now he only looked in the trunk. He wasn't good at folding, not like Cody who, despite being a total slob, folded everything precisely in his drawers, even his socks, lining up the heels. He respected this about Cody; he knew where that tiny need to fold resided, it was somewhere between the sternum and the belly button—Toby had that place, too, only instead of folding he *needed* to listen. He knew it was the same, just as he knew they both remembered all the words of their secret language, even when they pretended it was forgotten, baby stuff.

Looking in the trunk, Toby was careful with Linsey's things: her sweater that was new and smelled like the store; her little cloth-covered poetry books, e.e. cummings she'd shown him and she'd tried to explain; her letter from her ex-boyfriend, not really ex, really still her boyfriend, Timmy, which she'd slipped into a little gap between the trunk lining and the lid. He knew it would be in there. He liked reading it and felt awful for it, the way scratching a mosquito bite until all the skin around it comes off in a satisfying wad and it bleeds and stings like mad but doesn't itch so much anymore feels good. *Linny*, it started. *My Linny, you know I love you. You know I have to talk to the other girls at school and I have to be friends with them and you know sometimes I might even go out with one of them just like I know you might even go out with that bean-head Markos Hubbard because he's been after you for, like, the entire duration of your glorious life, but, Linny, we're going to be together, you know that, I know that . . .* Sometimes Toby stopped here. Sometimes he read the whole thing, and tried not to imagine the things Timmy said he wanted to do with her, sex things they had planned in explicit detail—he'd heard some of this on the phone, too—and it made him hard and embarrassed and now he got a little hard just reading the first part so he stopped before it hurt.

Yesterday when he came to the house, right after camp, the detective had said, "Talk to everyone you know." Toby had been listening from the top step. Cody had been playing the hijacking game on Xbox that was too violent for them to own, but which he'd borrowed from stupid Banks, whose parents bought him anything he ever wanted just because he was good at football. Toby felt sick when he watched the boxing game, too much blood everywhere, too much hitting.

There was such a thing as too much violence, he knew that; he didn't understand why Cody thought things that were really really repulsive were cool at the same time. It wasn't like the maggots they'd seen in a dead squirrel on Cedar Court. That kid next door—Geo—the one Cody called weird—Geo was always taking pictures and he was there just six inches from the awful swarming mass. They were doing their job, even if their numerousness and motion seemed repulsive; they were of the world, they were science, they were decomposition. The beating up didn't seem to have a reason.

He worried that something like that might have happened to Linsey. He imagined it, he imagined her being hit. He hated how it made him feel, tight chest, head hot, but he still imagined it. Her face bruised, her arms pinned, Linsey crying. And he hated that it was kind of exciting to think about the things that could have happened to her. He loved Linsey. He wanted her home. He was angry in the first place that she was going to college, and he was annoyed that he was supposed to keep secret the fact that she'd sneaked out to see Timmy at least five times this summer, even though they were supposed to be broken up, but he kept it a secret, because even though it might be important, if it wasn't, and he squealed, she might stop telling him things when she found out.

Linsey told him things she didn't tell anyone else, certainly not Cody, and not Mom, and even things she didn't tell Timmy. Sitting on his bed one afternoon—right after the breakup—Linsey pretended to help with his homework.

"Right," she said, bouncing on the bed with that look that said she would like to test the rules. "Imperfect fractions!"

"No, irregular verbs."

He liked it when she was silly. He didn't need help; they just liked their own occasional private world.

"Improper vowels!" she said, rising to her knees and bouncing more.

"No, immeasurable cookies."

"Cookies! Ooo!" Linsey bounded out his door. He could hear her taking the stairs, so much louder than her frame suggested. She returned with packets of chocolate chip cookies, the kind they gave out at games when it was their turn for snacks. Usually reserved for Cody's events.

"Cookies," she said. "I am very, very, very sad." She pouted at him, imp-like.

"Really?" Toby didn't like eating on the bed, crumbs would wake him later, so he sat on Cody's bed and opened the packet.

"No, yes," said Linsey. "I think Mom is crazy for breaking us up—you know, it's only because she and Dad couldn't manage, and she thinks we're like them, but we're nothing like them." She shook her cookie bag.

"Don't crush them," said Toby, thinking of the crumbs. He patted Cody's bed, a suggestion.

Linsey didn't get up. She tossed the bag to him as he finished his.

"Mom and Dad broke up, like, three times, and got back together before she met Frank."

He didn't like it when she called Dad Frank, but she always did. It was Mom and Frank, which made them sound unmatched. He didn't like the idea that Mom could have ever taken Joe back—that his dad, and he and Cody, weren't inevitable. He tore open the second cookie bag and let her continue.

"Dad was always meeting girls on shoots." Toby didn't like Joe—his hair was long and goopy and he spoke slowly to Toby and Cody, as if they were slightly stupid.

"And he's cute enough to get it on with some of the pro soccer women—the straight ones—even though he's so much older."

Toby wondered whether *get it on* meant sex, but he just nodded. Linsey flopped back on his bed.

"I would have done it with Timmy. I love Timmy." She coughed a little, like a fake cry. She was making it all sound so light, when he knew she really meant it, about the sadness. *Get it on* meant sex, then.

Last year, Linsey had told him it hurt to get her period. She told him what girls liked when they were kissed; she even kissed him once, because he'd begged, called it practice, but then made him swear they'd never do it again because it was too weird and he was her sister. Half sister, he said. Still, she'd said, her mouth purple inside and too sweet from the grape gum they'd both been chewing. "But don't let your mouth get quite that soft, it's too soggy." They never did that again, and they never talked about it, either, and sometimes Toby wasn't sure it had actually happened.

He called Linsey's cell phone. She'd promised she'd always answer for him, unless she was at a concert or in a class or something. He'd called her once when he stayed home sick from soccer camp and Mom had gone into the city for the morning and the house had been too weird, all empty. He'd called her once when he lost his key and Cody had gone over to the Banks's house and she came home from school to let him in, even though she missed chemistry and it was AP. Now she was going away, and if he needed her and called, she might be in a more important class, like something premed, which she was thinking about even though everyone thought she was going to be a special-education teacher. Cornell was far away, too far for him to take a bus to visit her. He'd wanted her to go to NYU like she'd always said she would, but when she finally visited, she didn't like it. Or maybe she wanted to get away from them.

He'd called her four times since yesterday, since they knew she was missing; the voice mail picked up right away. The second time he left a message, "Lins, dude, where are you? I know you're probably busy or something but call home, okay? Mom's kind of going nuts."

After Cody said that stupid thing about Linsey and the room, Mom came downstairs and didn't even yell at Cody for eating cookie dough off the sheet on the floor. She had a red spot on her arm, as if someone had given her an Indian burn. She dialed Dad's number and talked to him with her hand held over her mouth, though the boys could hear her if they tried. Cody didn't; he was watching a rerun of *The Simpsons*.

Toby tuned out the comforting, ridiculous voices and heard his mother say, "Let's hire someone, anyone." He knew she must mean private detective, but he also imagined a new babysitter, a sort of Mary Poppins character who would sweep him off his feet, out to the roof. They'd sing. Cody didn't like Mary Poppins, said she was boring.

"Myself," said his mother, her hand obscuring her mouth but not Toby's ears. "I hurt myself. Not them. Never them."

Both times the detective had come, yesterday and again this afternoon, Toby listened to everything he said, everything he could hear. He listened a lot; it was almost like a hobby. He listened in sometimes when Linsey, or Mom, or even Cody talked on the phone. He had this cool radio thing that could intercept a phone conversation—cell phones, portables. He said he used it for walkie-talkie stuff with his brother, but it was mostly for listening. It wasn't that he was a snoop, it was more that he was greedy for information about the world. And about Linsey, whom he loved, perhaps a little more than he ought to.

The detective's nose was disgusting. He was a youngish guy, younger than Toby's mom for sure, maybe younger than Miss Elephanten, the teacher he would have this year, fifth grade, who had black hair and teeth that were too white, everyone said she used Whitestrips, but they still liked her because she had a gentle voice and let them leave for recess early if they finished their math. The detective said Linsey had probably just run away, but she was going to Cornell so soon, it seemed ridiculous. Besides, Toby knew Linsey wouldn't want to do that to their mother; she wouldn't do that to him, either. Linsey let him sleep in her bed sometimes; she sang to him at the doctor's office when he had to get the allergy injections, lots of them, and he kept thinking about the needle coming into his skin, breaking it, pushing in past the layers and too close to the bone, and he wanted to throw up or wanted to run, but Linsey sang to him, silly kids' songs, "Kumbaya," some Beatles songs he liked even though the Beatles were cool for Linsey but not for him; she sang the alphabet song when she ran out, and "Alligators All Around," which she'd sung in his preschool as a visitor. Linsey had a great voice, Linsey could've gone into music if she wanted, but she didn't. The detective asked about boyfriends and his mom told him everything, even about the drugs, and the detective made little grunting noises and Toby imagined the sweat on his nose cumulating, coming together into a giant droplet, splattering on the notes he took with a leaky ball-point on a metal clipboard.

The detective had talked to Toby, and Cody, each alone in their room. He said things like, "You should tell me anything you know—anything that might be helpful," and Toby looked at the nose, the nose, the nose, and said, "I don't know anything my parents didn't already tell you." Later he thought about that, about how the detective might know he had been listening in because of that, about how he did know something they didn't—he knew she still loved Timmy. And he knew she had taken some of Mom's Valium, almost all the pills, that she'd wrapped them in a little wad of plastic wrap and stashed them along with her birthday money (tens and twenties and a single fifty-dollar bill) from the grandmother they didn't share, and two stubby candles and a matchbox inside the weird wooden box carved with monkeys on the lid that her father had given her from some trip—she kept it in her closet, behind her shoes. Toby didn't tell the detective he didn't like Joe, that he was always twisting and zipping his jackets, zip, unzip, zip, unzip, a very untidy, insectlike sound, as he waited on the front porch for Linsey. Sometimes he didn't even get out of the car. Toby liked him less than any of the boyfriends, because Linsey liked him more. He didn't tell the detective Linsey had a fight with her father the day before she left. And he didn't tell him, either, that the monkey box with all the money and the pills was gone.

She had called him last week from a party at Ian Cronin's house, her voice fat with alcohol. Actually, she'd texted him first. She wrote *I kissed Markos Love forever, L.* It was cruel, but sometimes if Linsey drank she was ridiculously affectionate and sometimes she was mean, it was just the way she was, a little too much of either side of herself. She'd called afterward, crying.

"If you don't want to lose me," she said. "Let's get married. Let's elope," she said. He knew a small part of her actually meant it, but mostly Linsey was too smart for all of this. She would walk home even though Cronin lived at least two miles from her house; she wouldn't drive drunk, she would never cheat at a game, she would write him a text if she even kissed someone, like Markos, and even though they were broken up.

"You're drunk," he said. "And if you kiss Markos now and someone else freshman year and then still want to be with me, we'll get back together over the summer." It was awful, but it would be worse if he tried to keep her—he couldn't fight her mother and he couldn't fight her free will or she'd grow too small for him; they'd grow too small for each other.

"You don't mean that," she said. "Just because my parents were stupid doesn't mean we are. Just because we're young doesn't mean we can't actually love each other. I'm done. I kissed Markos. That's it for kissing random boys; I only want you."

He had tried to talk her down. He offered to pick her up but she said no. He got off the phone and vomited, then he went running past Cronin's house in case she was still there, but she wasn't.

If he saw her, he would want her too much, and he couldn't make good choices.

It was all about making good choices.

And now her mother had called and asked about Linsey and his first thought was that he was supposed to meet her somewhere, was supposed to run away with her—she wasn't supposed to do it without him. He'd been up all night digging through his box of notes from Linsey, looking through old texts and e-mails.

Linsey didn't run away, no matter how much she thought she loved him; she had too much sense of self-preservation. She might kiss Markos, but would she sleep with a stranger? No. Would she be playing hide-and-seek with him to see if he really cared as much as he said he did? All summer he'd been working two jobs—he was a day camp counselor and an assistant to this guy in town who called himself Mr. Computer Dude, who set up home systems and made emergency calls to homes in desperate need of e-mail recovery—and he did this to save money to visit Linsey during Thanksgiving, when he had a week off and she had only two days, so he had a plane ticket and a rental car reserved to go visit her in Ithaca. It was just months. Just countable weeks. Just countable infinity.

Once, they'd been having one of those relentless conversations about whether love plus lust was greater than or less than the sum of love plus proximity—she called it love math—and she stopped his calculations of the distance between different airports that would be between them at their schools—and put her hand over his mouth. Usually, that would warrant a playful bite, but it was a week before they broke up, and he knew it was coming, a low-pressure system. He kissed her hand instead.

"What worries me," she said, "is that your love is a countable infinity. It can be measured even though it's infinite. You can use it in an equation." They were in her family room—no one else was home on a Saturday afternoon and the light licked the floorboards. He wanted to be inside her.

"Nah," he said. "For you, beyond measure." He'd been thinking that he wanted to taste other parts of her, the crook of her arm, her inner thigh. His mind was bored but his body wasn't and for this he felt a vague and uncomfortable guilt.

"No," she said. "My love for you is an uncountable infinity. It's not your fault, and it's not my fault, and I'm not sure you should buy that ticket."

It made him angry; it was an assumption. He wished he

could say something about disrespect but instead he said, "No way, I bought it already," and started pulling her T-shirt up over her head. His body was uninterested in change and anticipation—it wanted, and now. He hadn't imagined she would take her mother's mandate, just one week later.

Now he was supposed to leave for California, and even though she'd given him up, she was holding him back. He was alone in the house, and he missed her so much he felt as though he were wearing a lead apron at the dentist's. A pile of lead aprons, his chest crushed. He called his uncle and he called the airline and he stopped imagining the "Welcome, Timmy!" sign he'd been expecting at the airport, his uncle's square artistic handwriting a quiet public celebration of this huge thing he was doing—moving cross country, leaving his hometown, leaving Linsey.

The thought of someone else touching her—someone hurting her, someone taking her—made bile rise into his mouth. He couldn't leave her, because she was missing. He changed his flight to tomorrow and charged the fee to his mother's credit card—she could help out for once. Then he grabbed his bike from the garage and headed over to Linsey's house, dreading facing Abigail, but motivated by the thought of having some conversation with Toby, whom he'd missed, who always had some interesting angle on things, who might know the password to Linsey's laptop, so Timmy could put his Mr. Computer Dude skills to work and try to find her.

Two blocks away from the house, he felt the wavering. Abigail made him feel especially guilty, made him feel like he was the source of all sins. It wasn't entirely her fault; it was as though she secretly sensed the weak parts of him that wanted to appear strong, as though she knew he was still an unformed man.

The kid with the camera was standing a little too far into the street, his face behind the lens. Timmy didn't know anyone who used a film camera anymore, just this kid. He slowed his bike.

"Hey, Geo," he said. "You should watch for cars."

"I am," said the boy, turning his lens to Timmy. Timmy could feel the focus. The kid seemed to see without looking directly.

Timmy had known Geo since the boy rode his Big Wheels down Cedar Court and over by Linsey's house. He was always making art, and he'd been in the Super Science Saturdays program Timmy taught for three winters at the Campus Center in the high school. They'd made a battery together; they'd built a robot that smashed pegs into holes; they'd shared disastrous mushed origami projects and had been both serious and full of laughter.

"But there are cars," said Timmy, scooting forward until his face was right in the lens, laughing.

"Ooo, that was almost good," said Geo. "You came too close, though."

"You're taking pictures of my zits?"

Geo lowered his camera and his head both. "No," he said.

"I'm kidding. Hey, Geo, I know you take a lot of pictures. Any chance you have some of Linsey? It's just that we're kind of looking for her." He was wearing his camp-counselor hat, his conciliation.

Geo fiddled with his lens again.

"I might; I could look."

"Text me, okay? I'm in the directory—you know, from school—your sisters should have it." The sisters were always mysterious, a small tribe of beauty. The boy was smart, though; he might even have some recent shots. He leaned forward and touched Geo's shoulder. Geo was wearing a red cotton sweater even though it was hot out. He shrugged at the touch, but Timmy could tell he was happy to be included.

"I will."

"Onward!" said Timmy, smiling, though he wasn't, not really. He was scooting down the street like a reluctant toddler on a trike.

6½ SYCAMORE STREET

Sometimes, she noticed how gruesome his little place was, the microwave, the stained sink, the bathroom where he showered wearing flip-flops because the shower floor was mottled with a yellow and blue mold. Sex with him was so thorough— it used all of her, it temporarily erased her. He was so compelling on the bed, against the wall, his long thighs taut; the skin around his eyes smooth; his cock itself, always alert for her; his lemony smell, despite his horrible diet, despite the filth of his surroundings. She would never have lived somewhere like this, even without money; her sheets were always clean, her shower floor was never moldy. When she was away from him, the idea of him, this kid in a smelly old garage who had a degree from Harvard and could hardly get dressed in the morning depressed her. She wasn't sleeping with a kid like that. She'd stop right away. But then she was with him, and he was so sexual, so raw, and so immediate. It was like being with a toddler who wants wants wants; only you could satisfy the need without sippy cup or lollipop. All Jordan wanted was to make love to her, and it didn't get much better than sex with someone who had all that energy and hunger.

Reeva was always clean—she hated crumbs on counters and smudges on doorplates, but she harbored a desire to sink into thoughts and dreams, to let books pile up on end tables, even on the floor, piles of thoughts; she wanted to experience again the way she used to, sharp senses at the ready. She once had a job then at a used bookstore, shelving the new recruits, pasting little red price stickers on their backs, ringing up the uneven purchases—$5.43, $6.11—at the ancient push-button register in the front. Books smelled like dough in that book-shop, biscuit dough.

But then she lapsed into the ordinary, the office job she kept for three years before Steve was born, the peeling herself from bed early enough for all the necessary layers of shellac and moisturizer to keep her safe all day. Safe and beautiful. If left alone, really alone, Reeva wouldn't wear any of it. If left alone, she'd eat biscuit dough and read books and lie in bed all day. That's what she thought in the years of young chil-dren, the relentless years of nursing and diapers and night-time calls for her attention, her arms.

She was lured into real estate by a sign on a storefront agency office in town. She had been up for too many nights, for two or three years, it felt as if she hadn't slept in that long, and she was horrified by her own outgrown haircut, her lip-sticks too old to hold their oils, wasting away in a drawer. She was horrified by how used up she felt, so she wheeled baby Tina into the office and signed up for a course. For those years there was so much power for her in dressing up for open houses, for escaping her own laundry piles and unread cooking magazines for a Sunday open house. The thrill of a deal was better than sex—less messy, less exhausting; instead, she felt redeemed by joining home and owner, as if she was building something, not just feeding and changing and maintaining breath.

Charlie had convinced her to give up the brokering—too many Sundays away from home, and her cell phone always ringing. She didn't help them with their homework often enough. She'd complained about missing Tina's gymnastics, Steve's hockey, though she hadn't really wanted only that. Now she had all this time, the Sundays, but all the other days, too. Tina had long since quit gymnastics. His suggestion had seemed logical, but she missed the work, even if she didn't miss sitting in a vacant house that smelled of cat urine despite her quick batch of slice-and-bake cookies on a Sunday afternoon, dressed in a wool jumper and cold in November, clipboard, unnecessary fresh lipstick. Though it was the games and meets she mentioned, Johnny was the main reason she'd agreed to relinquish her job. He needed her too much for her to be filling empty houses.

Now she had this time, a whole lapful of time, and did she go back to bed after everyone left for school? Did she tend peonies in the garden and make cookies and lie on the couch with novels? No. She went to Library Friends meetings. Charlie sometimes bought her new hardcover novels at Christmas, and she read them, dutifully falling in love with reading again, but at bedtime, staying up later than she'd intended, while Charlie read his political thrillers or his secret stash of science fiction with fleshy women on the front. They looked like Greek statues, all drape and exposure, all suggestion of solidity. Now she had the time, and how did she spend it? At the gym. Every day of the week she worked to keep herself in shape. She wasn't sure, sometimes, why she did it. Maybe it was for Charlie, partly; maybe it was because she felt all her power leaking from her as her body sagged. Maybe because having those children had used her, if not using her up, at least wearing her out. Sometimes she ate too much. Sometimes she stopped at the bakery to get the kids a treat—picking out cream horns and sprinkle cookies and nut-crusted frosted brownies, bad as Jordan, maybe another thing about him she coveted, and sometimes she came home and ate everything out of the white box, too impatient to untie the string, so she bit through it. Sometimes she did all this without really noticing until there was only one thing left, or two, and then she ate them as if she needed to hide the evidence. She took out the trash, Tina and Steve's job, alternating, and soon enough Johnny's, too, though she didn't look forward to helping him learn that ritual, learn over and over by doing, like teaching an old person who's forgotten how to use the bathroom.

She embarrassed herself by thinking about Johnny this way, and she embarrassed herself by eating the treats, but she also needed them. It was only once a month or so. She made up for it at the gym, day after day. Sometimes it felt good when she was done, but she never enjoyed the actual doing, the bike, the mountain climber, the rower, the machines, the

Pilates class. There were frightening women in there, women who had been dancers and whose fifty- or sixty-something bodies stretched out obscenely, who worked away at the invisible flab on their upper arms as if evil, as if the devil itself were manifest in the tiniest portion of flesh. She wasn't insane this way. She had her spots of softness, and she didn't hate them, and neither did Charlie, and now, neither did Jordan, whom she allowed to investigate, bit by bit, though often they had sex with most of their clothing on.

After the first time with Jordan, she was sitting across the dinner table from Charlie, and she couldn't hear her own voice when she spoke. All the children were elsewhere, and she felt exposed. If she said anything, lust would fall out of her mouth like a fat slab of tongue at the butcher. It silenced her, what she'd done, it made her subhuman, because she'd done this to her husband. They were having an ordinary conversation—about that babysitter Linsey Hart.

"I can't believe that girl is old enough to apply for college," she'd started, only now she couldn't tell whether she'd said it, or just thought it. "I can't believe soon Tina will be applying to colleges—before we know it." At least she thought she'd said it. In her mind, her words whooshed and thudded, like an organ about to cease its relentless work.

"We should plan another college tour," said Charlie. He was putting too much butter on his dinner roll, a fat pat, a tablespoon at least. *He is thinking of the children while I cheat on him. I am pathetic.*

"I can't manage that," is what she thought she said. Or

else she said she couldn't bear it, either way, her mouth felt cottony and useless.

Charlie didn't notice anything.

"You think? Maybe next summer?" He stuffed the bread into his mouth, butter pat first. He could do this, and yet if he left her he'd still find someone new. His mouth was rich and wet and her mouth was dry, used.

"I don't know," she said. Or thought she said.

"Okay," said Charlie. He wasn't even listening. She could open her mouth and birds could spill out onto the table, mockingbirds, crows, raptors, and he'd just get up and leave his dish on the counter and go sit down in his permanently pleated work pants and beige cashmere sweater reading his travel magazine and she'd never know what he was thinking—because he could never know what she was thinking.

Later that evening her ears popped, as if she had been in an elevator, on an airplane, climbing mountains. She could hear her own voice yelling up to Johnny that he needed to take his socks and Cheez Doodles bowl off the couch. She could hear herself telling her husband good night.

Sex with Jordan made her disgusted as much as it thrilled her. It was not unlike eating all the cream horns. It was decadent and she needed it, or at least she told herself she needed it, she told herself she couldn't stop, only now she might stop, she might go cold turkey from Jordan, she might do the right thing after doing the wrong thing for so long. Perhaps she didn't want to be with Jordan—perhaps she wanted to be him, all inhibition lapsed. Jordan didn't care what the neighbors thought. He paid his rent and parked his car in back. He ate as he wished and called his parents when he felt like it; she didn't know whether Jordan ever felt guilty. She wondered whether cigarette smokers, the heavy regulars, felt like she did. Repulsed and in need. Twice, when he couldn't get off work, she let him take her into his stockroom at Starbucks, locking the door, pushing into her as she leaned against a shelf rich with giant silvery coffee bags. She came out of the store smelling more of smoky coffee than of sex.

It had been two weeks since Linsey, carrying Johnny, had passed by Jordan's windows, looked in at her squalid little affair, and maybe she saw and maybe she didn't. Now Linsey was missing. How long had it been—since she didn't show up yesterday, or longer? Had she simply run away with her boyfriend? Reeva was well past her teens and still experienced the urgencies of the body.

Last night the stepfather had canvassed the neighborhood with flyers, MISSING GIRL. It was strange, almost as if they were advertising a play, or a garage sale. Linsey in black and white on bright pink paper, festive paper. Mr. Stein had rung the bell this morning after the boys left and while Reeva was upstairs in the bathroom, checking to be sure she'd taken her birth control pills, sitting on the toilet counting out the little pillows of drug. She'd told Jordan she'd meet him, but she was having second thoughts. Last night, Charlie had wanted to make love. He'd grunted and put his hand in her hair and laid his arm over her waist like a man claiming an entire territory. It was both touching and horrible, because Reeva's body betrayed her—she became aroused. She'd allowed it, the ordinary sex of a married couple. She'd come, thinking for a minute that Jordan's mouth was on her own, only Charlie was far gentler than Jordan, his teeth never clacked painfully against hers, he never kissed the insides of her thighs, he never pushed against her too hard.

The doorbell rang and Reeva stood up to look down through the waxy-leafed magnolia in the front yard. She could see the top of a man's head, and then, as she watched without going downstairs, he turned away from her door and walked on to the next neighbor's house.

The flyer stuck in her screen door had a handwritten note on the back, "If you know anything—"

Linsey was only a few years older than Tina, and so much more mature. Better, she thought, feeling disloyal. Gentler— at least she seemed that way with Johnny. But had Reeva been wrong to trust Linsey with her Johnny? What if she had told him things he shouldn't know? What if she was like Reeva herself, a reverse geode, all crystal and value outside, but dun, flat-faced, flawed within? Reeva didn't believe that Linsey would run away—it was probably the mother's fault.

Reeva left the car in the driveway and walked along Syca-more Street, listening to the hissing of cicadas in the trees and sprinklers making wet green paint of the grass. She walked back through the woods behind the cul-de-sac and arrived early, despite her best intentions, despite her husband's quick, soft "Thank you, beautiful" in the morning before he left the bed, as if that made up for everything. She carried a bottle of wine she'd grabbed from under the wood island in the kitchen—she didn't care what it was or how expensive. Jordan liked drinking with her, and though it was midmorning, she wanted to taste wine on his tongue. She imagined it on the walk, holding the bottle inside her arm like a girl carrying her books to school.

"Hi," said Jordan, standing at the door. He had chocolate on the corner of his mouth and she reached up to wipe it away, right there, outside, visible.

"Inside," he said.

"Since when do you care?" Reeva wanted to taste it now, and she licked the corner of his mouth as he shut the door. She pushed him on the bed.

"Hey, you're full of ambition today," he said.

"What's that supposed to mean?"

Jordan took a pink piece of paper from his pocket, unfolding the leaflet—Linsey Hart's face, the clean lines of her chin, the long hair in black and white.

"I know this girl," he said. "Or at least, I knew her in middle school. It's weird. She never seemed like the runaway type. She even asked me out once. Brave little thing. I wonder what happened."

"How could you have been in middle school with her?" Reeva took off his T-shirt. It smelled of crushed grass and

— 111 —

lemony sweat. He'd started running, he told her, he wanted to get into shape. She'd told him she liked his shape, and she did, the lean lines, no worse for a thousand brownies. She pushed her hand into his waistband. She was here for sex, after all, and part of her wanted it over with, part of her wanted her body to stop asking for it, stop aggressing her into this ridiculous situation. She got up and looked for a corkscrew on his counter, the one she'd lent him, one of the six or seven they owned. Dirty socks, candy wrappers. What was she doing here? The kitchen smelled like mildew and old cheese. The girl asked him out in middle school. It didn't make sense.

"Maybe I skipped a grade."

She found the corkscrew under a doily—she had no idea why Jordan had a doily, maybe his grandmother made them—and poured the wine into the two cleanest paper cups she could find.

"Still, you'd have missed her in middle school by years."

"Maybe I skipped more than one grade," said Jordan. The wine spilled down his chest and he rested his cup on a shelf, took a swig from the bottle of pinot noir.

"Excuse me?" Reeva looked at his eyes, so young, so clean, sort of horrible. He put down the bottle and reached for her, sliding his hands inside her jeans, reaching inside her and cupping her ass, always fluid in his sexual motions. Reeva felt it, but she was still calculating.

"Linsey Hart is only seventeen," she said.

"Almost eighteen," he said.

"Only *almost* eighteen." He kissed her hard as she said it, but she pushed him away. "So how old are you, Jordan?"

Jordan didn't stop massaging her, his hands between her legs, his mouth on her breast through her T-shirt, which was really Tina's T-shirt; she'd borrowed it and just an hour ago it had made her feel sexy and now she realized how absurd she looked. It was a tight V-neck. It was pink and girly and she was not a girl.

A girl was missing. Where was Tina right now? At camp, she hoped, worrying about her hair. She couldn't be approaching this same sort of life, this debauchery, this embarrassment. Her daughter wasn't *stained.*

"How old?"

"Fine," said Jordan. "I'm twenty." He pushed at her hips, grabbing, maneuvering her onto the bed. The sex scent rose from the sheets. Did he ever wash his sheets? His mouth was on hers but it felt hard and wrong.

"Almost," he said.

Reeva stared at his forehead. There was still a little chocolate, over by his ear. She shoved him away. He groaned and pressed her down on the bed.

"I like that," he said.

"You're fucking nineteen years old?"

"No," he said and grinned. "You're fucking nineteen years old."

"Very funny," said Reeva, trying to stand up. "You can't be nineteen years old."

"Right," he said. "I can't drink." He picked the bottle up

from the floor and pressed it obscenely between her legs. This would've excited her just yesterday, she thought. She was that base.

"You can't drink," she repeated.

"And I can't buy booze, either."

"Jesus Christ."

"Jesus good or Jesus bad?"

"You can't buy alcohol," she said, as if it mattered.

"I have to get older women to bring it to me." He tried to reach for her breast but she slapped at his hand. "Don't be like that," he said.

Older women. She felt it physically, her face melting, the old face beneath the plastic new one; she was an old lady, and he was nineteen years old. She got up and backed toward the door.

"Only old ladies with great tits." He grabbed at her, suddenly inelegant. Nineteen years old. A prodigy in more ways than one, but still a baby, she was sleeping with a baby, she was a horror. He had referred to her tits. She hated that word. She hated this smelly little room, but he was pulling her back to the bed, his hot hairless hands on hers, thinking she was playing, how could he think that? He was pulling her back to him; his fingers dug into her crotch, pushing her jeans down. Nineteen years old.

"Cellophane," she said.

He kept going, as if he hadn't heard her, but she knew he'd heard it, and she knew he knew.

"Cellophane," she said again. "Cell-oh-phane."

Jordan put his hands up in the air, surrender. He wouldn't look at her. He lay back on the bed and stared at the ceiling. She'd seen that ceiling. Knotty pine beams, gray cobwebs, a jagged crack in the paint over by the door.

He lay there while Reeva gathered her things—the corkscrew; a novel she'd lent him, *Life of Pi*, which Charlie had given her; her underwear from a few days ago, crusty with sex; she took the bottle from between his feet. It would make her weird and conspicuous, walking up Sycamore Street with an open bottle before noon. And she knew it was over and she only hoped he wouldn't tell. He wouldn't tell. He was nineteen. She was ancient. She thought of Charlie's heavy arm and she knew she was going home to him, to their quiet shipwreck, to see what could be salvaged. The captain, her Charlie, didn't even know they were underwater, halfway between the whitecaps and the bottom of the sea.

She walked out of his door without looking around first, without being furtive, with nothing to hide. And maybe he saw her and maybe he didn't, but down the woods path, Mr. Leonard was walking through the oaks and maples, still at the height of their greens, pushing his antique bike with one hand, holding something pink in the other. It wasn't until later that Reeva remembered that silhouette, that strange juxtaposition, old man, pink cloth, and wondered, and filled in the missing puzzle pieces. In the dappled light of her memory, he was holding Linsey Hart's pink sweatshirt as if it belonged to him now.

24 SYCAMORE STREET

He hadn't been sleeping; he hadn't been eating; his gut was killing him, the cancer eating him from inside. He had moments of daily respite, and he spent those outside, walking, or on his bike. He felt it spreading exponentially, and it was both a gripping hurt and a fascination. It was as if he could see it in color, hear the cancer cells like notes, piling and growing on each other, a movement, an overture, a finale. He'd been lying in his bed, on his back, brittle as a bone, playing measures over and over, unable to stop. Borodin, Debussy. Handel's *Dixit Dominus,* the soprano soloist answering the violins, a sinuous, winding conversation, lines like the floating of a feather, back and forth and down in soft stair steps, though air. Sometimes he played pieces his hands knew, but more often it wasn't for piano, sometimes it was a bit of the Brahms requiem, the *Zigeunerlieder,* Hungarian gypsy songs. Back on one limb of his family tree, his father's side, there had been Hungarian gypsies—they sang to him through the music, raucous, gorgeous voices. Sometimes it was Prokofiev, Verdi's *Macbeth,* sometimes *Aida.* He hardly ever listened to recordings these days, his old turntable with the stylus that floated in a viscous mercury sea was off balance, and he didn't want to take it in to the one shop left that repaired turntables in Fair Lawn. They would keep it overnight at least, and he needed it to be home, even if it wasn't working. The music kept him up, effective as the chattering of parrots; for all its lyricism, it broke his thoughts in an unbearable cacophony.

He didn't know exactly what they were after when they came, but he did know he was safer playing the notes more logical than any conversation. They knocked on the door at eleven PM, a posse, a little flock of men with uniforms and nightsticks, with huge silver flashlights. He was wearing a gown, his mother's, champagne silk, open in the back like a maw, and he saw himself in the mirror, so he tugged it to the floor, never mind that they might see through the stained glass. He grabbed his robe and wrapped it around his body, all bruise from within. The gown rested like a half-melted woman in the hallway. Perhaps he'd worn it for two days, though he didn't remember putting it on, he rarely remembered putting it on, only that he was safer in his mother's dresses, that he used them when he was most lost to anchor himself to the corporeal world. He hadn't needed to leave the house after his Wednesday library trip; it had rained and he hadn't felt like biking or walking, only drinking tea and playing his music or thinking his music, and what crime was there in not leaving his house? For a minute he thought they were coming about the dresses. But what crime was there in a dying man wearing his dead mother's dresses? And who should care? He was almost old, after all. He was dying. He'd felt old for decades now, since his aunt was gone, older still since he lost the job, older still since he'd lost the order inside his body, since he was being consumed.

He opened the main door and they spoke through the screen.

"Mr. Leonard?" It was the one he knew, Beau, from around the corner on Pine, only there was nothing casual in his posture, nothing that made Mr. Leonard even think he might offer coffee to this man. The light was horrible, so he shaded his eyes.

"That's a little bright," he said.

"Oh, is it?" asked another one of them, whose chest was huge, pigeon huge, puffed, his voice too round for someone older than ten, Mr. Leonard thought. He held his beam closer, like a sword, like a challenge.

"That's enough, Pete," said Beau, lowering his own beam.

"Of course," said Mr. Leonard. "It's halogen, isn't it? Or one of those mercury-vapor lights? You want to come in?" He was humming as he spoke. An old habit. The kind of habit that used to make people think he was strange. In fifth grade, humming the angry rhythms of Mars from Holst's *The Planets* while he gave his report on the solar system. It wasn't his fault; his mind couldn't separate one from the other.

"We have some questions, sir. You know about this missing girl?" It was Pete. His beam was lowered, but still erect, an offending object, still threatening.

"Linsey Hart was my next-door neighbor," said Mr. Leonard, suddenly alert.

Pete grunted. Beau shuffled, then stepped inside. Mr. Leonard backed up. The lights.

"I'd like you to sit," Beau said to Mr. Leonard.

"I'd rather stand," said Mr. Leonard, thinking that his robe had a hole where the belt loop was worn. Too much tugging taut over the years. They all gazed at the gown on the floor. They stepped around it. When it was off, it was ridiculous to imagine he had been wearing it.

"Sit," said Pete, and gave him a little shove. It didn't hurt. "Christ," Pete punctuated Mr. Leonard's collapse, and turned back to the hallway, tapping the dress with his toe. "What the hell is *that*?"

"A gown," said Mr. Leonard.

"Calm down, Pete," said Beau.

There were four men in his living room, and he looked at the piano longingly. He stepped past Beau and Pete and someone else, whose face he couldn't see under the hat brim, hat still on, very rude of him, and sat on his bench, reaching the single safe shore in the house. He had no slippers, and suddenly his feet were very cold; his toenails felt as though they were freezing off his body.

"I don't like that you said she *was* your next-door neighbor," said Beau. "I would think you might say she *is* your next-door neighbor."

"Christ, Beau," said the third man from under his hat. "You gonna lead him or what?"

He had a high tenor tone; he sounded like a child. All these children in his house, at his piano. Mr. Leonard wanted to introduce their recital. Instead, he fingered the keys, not pressing enough to sing them. But he heard them just the same, the melodic line from *The Damnation of Faust*.

"I said *was*." He was humming. Stop, he thought, but he couldn't. Maybe they could hear him and maybe not. Maybe they heard the music and maybe they heard the words or maybe they just heard what they wanted to hear.

"Because she's going off to college," he finished. But it didn't matter, Pete was holding up their search warrant, and the two men whose names he didn't know were already moving things, his things, pressing their thick fingers between the spines of his bound scores, tearing at the records as if they might house something other than moments, something other than performance, something other than simple music.

"What are you looking for?" he asked Beau, who was gently opening the piano. He couldn't bear that, it was like someone was prying open his mouth. Even Beau, who had sat at that piano.

"I'm not supposed to say," said Beau, wincing as he dropped the lid on his own fingers. At least there was no wooden crash, thought Mr. Leonard.

"No," said Mr. Leonard. "I suppose not, but perhaps I could help you if you told me."

Beau considered this for a minute. "Maybe," he said.

They weren't going to find it until they told him, and they

weren't going to tell him tonight. What they were after was buried in the side yard beneath the slowly dying dogwood, wrapped around the tiniest of bones.

For a while, before his father died, Mr. Leonard thought he might be a composer. He was performing then, competing, medium-size gigs, but nothing beyond accompanying Met competition finalists in concerts in the park in the New Jersey suburbs, or his own big solo pieces in small college concert halls, his audience half retirees, half faculty, some of whom brought papers to grade while they listened. Once, he played at Nordstrom's near Christmastime. He didn't like that, felt oppressed by the stringent Easter lily perfume and the clattering of boot heels as they stepped off the bottom of the escalator, just missing the rhythm of the moving stairs. He'd called his father, because he started having music dreams, music he couldn't identify, even by humming the bars over and over, which usually eventually found them their rightful names in the file drawers of his mind. He'd been teaching on and off at the Manhattan School of Music. He liked the intimate conversations with students in the tiny, mouse-and-cinnamon-scented practice rooms. Mostly upright pianos, mostly windowless rooms, so they had to make windows and light of the music. He hardly ever worked them through scales then, even beginners got simple pieces, because even at its worst, the beautiful bones of the music were better than the broken rhythms of simple scales, accompanied by the thunks and sighs of metal expanding inside the radiators.

"I'm thinking," he said to his father, who was in Vienna, finishing an opera season. "I might go in a different direction."

"South?" his father said. "Never trusted Florida."

"No, I mean with the teaching." Of course, his father was teasing. His father didn't like to talk about Mr. Leonard's music, only his own. He'd begin, and his father would overtake the conversation, as if they were in a race toward final punctuation.

"You know, those who can't do—" He didn't finish this old argument. Mr. Leonard never knew whether his father even wanted him to *do,* wanted to conduct his own son in some great Rachmaninoff concerto with the New York Philharmonic, standing ovations, no one could say there was any nepotism, Mr. Leonard having made it on his own, or whether his father would've been happier if his son had become an accountant, an orthodontist, anything but his own tortured successful road. Mr. Leonard knew his father took sixteen capsules every morning, heart pills, useless in the end, C and other vitamins, fish oil, Valium. He'd had the prescription since Mr. Leonard's mother's death, and he wondered whether his father had grown immune to the fog, because it never made him sleep, only move through the day instead of finding sticking points like flypaper in the corners of the room. The secret to his success.

"No," he said. "I mean, I like teaching, and I have to pay the rent, but I'm having these music dreams."

"Dreams of grandeur or dreams of measure?" His father breathed heavily into the phone, as if he was running in place while talking to his son. Mr. Leonard imagined the hotel room, ornate brass bed, thick brocade curtains, gold velvet upholstery, stainless, pine scented.

"Dreams of measure."

"You have two choices, write it down, or do your best to forget," said his father.

His adviser at Julliard told him he could take some more composition classes. He'd never loved them; he'd had one inspiring teacher at the beginning, then duds to follow, men trapped in their own simple rhythms, their own repeated tonics, I, I, I. Always leaning toward the minor keys, toward simple passions and dark clothing.

"No," said Mr. Leonard. "I know how to write them down, and I can hear more than three or four voices, it's orchestral. Not symphonies, I don't think. Or maybe, maybe just movements."

"You really need to take your time to become a composer," said his former adviser, chewing a toothpick. Mr. Leonard used to love the stuffy little office where they'd gone over his plans semester after semester, but he was done now, done with the room, done with the soft arms of study. It was all his own heavy wagon now, the music.

"No," said Mr. Leonard. "Not become. Already *be*."

"I disagree. You are already a musician, you were born a musician, but a composer is something to become."

"No," said Mr. Leonard, surprising himself. He hadn't

come to argue with his mentor. But he was thinking of his father, thinking of the way his father had never stopped *being* a conductor, a consummate musician, even the day after his mother died, when he gave a lecture at Tanglewood, a final talk on the history of dance music. His mother was dead, and Mr. Leonard lay in the narrow bed in the rental cottage, his mother's blue jeans, the only thing his father hadn't packed away, wrapped around him like a thick, grass-stained scarf. She'd worn them outside with him; they smelled of the backs of her knees. He had been waiting for his father to collect him, to make all the changes that were coming, the cleaving of the remaining two. But his cleaving was the other kind, apart. He'd gone into his music like Orpheus into the underworld and had never come up again. That last glance was banishment.

Mr. Leonard took a sabbatical from the teaching, and only performed the best-paying gigs. For six months he slept and woke and wrote the music of his dreams, but even though he heard them orchestrally, his pencil stopped after a melody and a single harmony, point and counterpoint—he couldn't replicate the grandeur of what he'd heard. He felt like a banished angel, as if he lost some senses between waking and sleep. When he woke, his head throbbed, his forehead felt as though it were splitting, a division between the lobes pressing outward from inside against his subcutaneous fat, the skin itself. His ear rang, a spontaneous high thrum, which started and stopped without warning. Mr. Leonard was being made ill by his own music. He sat at the little desk he'd bought at a yard sale in Queens, linoleum top, curved metal rim, a perfect round-edged rectangle of space, chips of mica in the yolk yellow surface, and he couldn't get past a scattering of notes. They looked like dots to him, just dots, for the first time in his life since he'd learned to read music—at age three, learning music as a second language, or first, concurrently with learning to read English—it made no sense to him. Poppy seeds, ants, buds, scabs, ellipses, the lines were vines, road divisions, hairs, guitar strings, flat lines, nothing, nothing. His head pulsed with the whining sound, with wanting the music he'd made, or had been given by God, if there was a God, then why was God torturing him?

When he told his father it wasn't working out, his father sighed into the phone. An abrasive sound, perhaps it would've sounded sad in person, but through the phone it sounded as though his father was hissing at him.

"Ah well," he said. "Ah well. I suppose those who can't do—"

"Fine," said Mr. Leonard. "I'll teach."

"No," said his father. "I was going to say, those who can't do what they were born to do might need a bit more ripening before they are ready to speak."

Mr. Leonard was so surprised by this almost encouragement he said nothing.

"Of course," his father finished, "those who can't do also teach. So go forth and teach, my son, go forth and teach."

"This is one weird asshole," Pete said, kicking at a pile of scores in the bedroom. The bed itself was full of music, of books and loose sheets, lying in the bedclothes like extra blankets. A hundred printed sheets of paper, fifty books, and pencils, and blank pieces of staff paper, and eraser crumbs from single notes written and erased. The ghosts of treble clefs and meter markings pressed into the staves, then gone, never right. On a table by the bed, there were apples in a bowl, letting loose the scent of sweet rot. Neat stacks of dried apricots, like a sculpture. Orange Stonehenge. Pete flicked at the fruit and it fell.

"His socks are all organized but his bed's all covered with this shit—" He kicked at the bedpost, his boot snapping a pencil.

"It's music, dude," said Carl, who was wishing he hadn't volunteered to come along on this search.

"Who the fuck listens to this anymore?" asked Pete, throwing the scores on the floor and kicking at them. He had reddish mud on his boot, and it fell off onto the worn Chinese carpet in little filthy rectangles. Carl knew Pete liked a little Christmas music, that he stopped at the mall to listen to the carolers in Nordstrom, that he didn't hate classical music. Carl had played clarinet in the marching band. He liked a little parade music; he liked the Messiah sings at his church. And so did Pete. They'd even listened to the classical station together once for about ten minutes, sitting in the Jeep on the downtown beat. Carl liked it when they had the Jeep—the seats were comfortable and the heater worked well without drying out your whole face. He thought about the Jeep to stay calm while he dug through the old guy's drawers with his gloves on. Looking for pink.

"You do, dude," said Carl. "I know you like music. It's not such a big deal, maybe this guy didn't do anything."

"It just makes me sick," said Pete, snapping on his gloves to dig through a pile of laundry like a fastidious kid searching for a lost coin in a pile of sand.

Carl looked under the bed; he went into the closet, which was naked except for one tuxedo and one blue suit hanging among the empty hangers like leafless trees. No loose floorboards. No hidden compartments. Just the smell of cedar and apricots and apple rot. The radiator began to hiss and clang.

"Hey," called Beau from downstairs. "Anything?"

"Another *gown*. Baby blue. I packed it up. Just ask him where he left the fucking sweatshirt," grunted Pete. He kicked the bedpost, and the thinnest sliver of oak cracked off like a toothpick.

Carl leaned over to pick it up. "Shit," he said. "Now I have a splinter." He sucked at his finger and slid the bit of wood into his pocket in the absence of any other evidence.

In the end they took him in. He wasn't an agitated subject, he was placid. He asked to bring his tweed hat and though he may've tapped his fingers in an annoying rhythm all the way into Hackensack in the squad car, he didn't protest. Which made Pete suspicious. Not Beau, Beau was suspicious of their own intentions. He noticed that Pete pushed Mr. Leonard into the car with a little too much force, so the old man bumped his head on the edge of the open door. He noticed that Mr. Leonard was pale and seemed confused, but he remembered Mr. Leonard at the piano, beside him on the bench, telling him to listen to the music in his head before he leaned into the keys, to hear what it was he meant to say before letting his fingers speak.

DAY THREE

She called Barq, the private detective they'd hired, once every two hours, except when she couldn't bear to wait the last two minutes, the last fifteen. He had been paradoxically patient and irritable with Abigail, listening to her minute confessions, her ideas, her redundant concerns. Just ten minutes ago she'd called and he picked up on the first ring.

"Mrs. Stein. I'm on my way to Providence."

"What—the boy she met from Brown at that party?" There had been a photograph—she'd sent a picture to Timmy of her too-pink face too close to Markos's on one side, and another boy's on the other. Markos told them he was a fellow Linsey had met when she visited Brown earlier in the year—Markos was uncomfortable reporting on the party, as if he were betraying her to Timmy, to Abigail when they asked. Finally he'd said that maybe Linsey had flirted with him, but maybe she hadn't—he had been too caught up in the party himself to notice.

"Timmy thinks that he just doesn't want to say he was drunk," Barq told her.

Timmy had let Barq copy everything from his phone—

which made Abigail guilty and grateful, both. Barq had shown her the cell phone picture, and she'd wondered when Linsey's cheekbones had gotten so clear, obscuring the sweet round of her cheeks. She'd looked at the boy from Brown and thought he looked like he kissed his mother's cheek; too innocent. But Barq was following up.

"Yes." He was calm. He needed a lozenge; his voice sounded phlegmy. "It may be nothing, Mrs. Stein. The police are canvassing your neighbors."

"Good," she said. "Because some of those people notice every car turning around in their driveways and who hasn't clipped their lawn." She felt mildly disingenuous—she pretended not to notice these things, but she did, too.

"And you might want to invite the boyfriend over, Timmy. He has been very cooperative and might open up to you."

"He hates me," she said. She felt a quick stab of sadness. It was her fault, all of it—she'd broken them up because she saw Linsey headed down the same path she had taken, but Linsey couldn't have taken that path; Linsey was too smart and too aware and besides, Timmy just wasn't Joe.

"But he doesn't hate Linsey," said Barq. "You should let me work and I'll let you know what I find."

"Okay," she said. It wasn't okay. "Have you checked—" But her pause had been too long.

"God bless," he said, as he always said, just before ending their calls. It made her nervous. Generally, Abigail was only used to the invocation of God at funerals, or in jest.

Abigail's days swam in slow motion, and passed in fast-forward. Linsey was her baby; Linsey was holding her twin baby brothers. Linsey had been stolen or had stolen herself away. Abigail couldn't decide whether her daughter could ever want to hurt her that much, but she knew the tearing apart from Timmy had left her daughter frayed. She used to feel as though she'd forgotten something; it was a sort of perpetual anxiety, something swallowed too soon before tasting, the lost idea, this side of eureka, or worse, toeing the line between safety and danger because she wasn't vigilant about watching her feet. In the months after she lost her son, Abigail woke and slept, a blurry line; she'd rather have been asleep all the time, to never wake, because when she woke, she remembered, over and over, she started, she stepped on falling ground, her son, her baby, she needed to get to him, only he was gone, not only gone, he was dead. She'd taken medication for a week or two, she never knew what it was, because Joe or her mother administered the capsules, and she took them, swallowed with a cup of juice like a child learning the art of pharmaceutical compliance. Afterward, she ate one cracker, or two spoonsful of applesauce, again, a child. "You need this for your stomach," Joe said, or her mother, "To keep your tummy from hurting." Her mother, she remembered why she loved her mother, those months. She didn't want to see her face, only to smell her woolly sleeves coming in close to tuck her in, her hand smooth and vaguely vanilla with Oil of Olay touching Abigail's own cheek, her shoulder, her back, leading her into the bathroom as if she'd forgotten where it was, needed help to walk. She had; she did.

Everything was different now. Abigail held off from calling her mother. This was temporary, this was missing, this
was not dead. She let herself think, once or twice, what her
Linsey would look like dead, only in her imagination, Linsey
was a baby again, with her first downy hair, a dove gray, her
eyes still blue, before they turned green, her knees still bent
from the cramped womb. She saw this dead Linsey twice, the
first night she had to sleep in the house without her daughter,
and last night, when it had been three days since Linsey left,
since she didn't hear the screen door sighing shut behind her,
since Linsey had not gone to work and had not come home.
She'd stayed up talking with Frank, loving his hands around
hers, loving the comfort of his voice, answering her thoughts
or just taking them in as she spilled everything out of her
mouth. She only ever did this with Frank—with everyone
else in the world she edited. Even the shrink she'd seen after
the lost baby, even when she was lost inside her own head she
still softened things, chose her words—Joe was very busy, not
selfish; Linsey was grieving in her own way, not shouldering
the weight of the house, a tiny superhero.

"I know the regular police aren't going to make this a pri-
ority, but you'd think Barq would step it up, I mean, we're
paying him so much—"

"Never mind that," said Frank. His hands smoothed hers,
as if he could lengthen the lifeline, the love line, with his fingers on her palms. "Money is money, but if you want, I'll call
him more often."

"I call him every two hours," she admitted. "I know I said

twice a day, but I can't help it—except at night; I let him have four or five hours to sleep. He does usually answer."

"You should call him as often as you want," said Frank.

"What we need is someone who works at it all the time," she said. She was working at it all the time. After Frank slept, she sat at the computer, researching abduction, runaways, looking online for any reference to Linsey's name, lurking in chat rooms where parents who lost their children grieved. She wouldn't look at those screens straight on, but she scanned them with her glasses off, hoping to see some clues, some ideas, something she hadn't tried yet.

"I think he's pretty good, but if you think we need to hire someone else—"

"What we need is to have her home."

"Yes."

"I haven't called Cornell again, I should call Cornell again. I just didn't want them to think I'm insane. I asked whether she'd checked in early, I didn't tell them anything. The first time. The second time I just asked when the dorms opened—"

"You can call Cornell again. Or I can call for you."

She sighed and kissed him. An ordinary kiss—extraordinary anxiety.

"You'd call Cornell?" she asked his regular breathing.

"I'll call Cornell," he said. "I'll call anyone you would like me to call."

She kissed him good night again, then thought to tell him what she'd read online, that highly successful teens are often very good at hiding drug problems. That sometimes they get caught when it's minor, but the relapses go unnoticed, because unlike the underachievers, the overachievers don't want to disappoint their parents by getting caught. She wanted to catch Linsey wherever she was, whatever she'd done; not that she suspected drugs any more than anything else. Catch her, arms wide, swing her into her own body like a child instead of an almost woman. Or throw herself onto whoever had taken her—or tempted her away. Abigail hadn't been vigilant—she couldn't know. She should know whether Linsey would run away so close to moving away—it didn't make sense, but then, she was at a vulnerable time, between the shelter of home and the sparser protection of college. It was all lost, her chance at being the fairy godmother, silver shadow in her daughter's childhood, protection, kindness, everything. She suspected that she'd forgotten to pay enough attention, that she'd lost her vigilance, that she'd done something to anger God, that he was taking another one away from her for her own faults. But Linsey didn't deserve to suffer; Linsey's sins were so minor they were hardly sins.

She had been in Linsey's room a dozen times; she'd unpacked and repacked the trunk, she'd examined the contents of closets and drawers, each time nervous, as if Linsey might be under the bed, watching. She knew this: she knew her daughter was alive. Then she didn't know. She had always envied the surety people had, or feigned enough to believe themselves—my baby will be a boy, I know it, or this will be a good year for the market, or I just know I'm going to meet the right man before I'm thirty—this was her friend Leslie, who was still single at thirty-nine, but who had changed her belief to before forty. It wasn't something she had. She hadn't known anything about her babies before they were born, except, of course, the details revealed about the twins by myriad tests, which she still didn't believe until they were born, and then, until they were two weeks old, and then, two months, two years. She didn't believe in the right to wake every day knowing your children are safe, how could she? She thought, at least, she could watch for them as best she could, in both the waking and dream worlds.

The neighbors were so full of certainties. Today the *Ridgewood Times* would come out with an article, she'd been told, about Linsey, and Ridgewood would, the world would know her daughter was gone. Maybe it would help. Maybe someone knew something, but Abigail felt as though the shades were being snapped up to reveal her family, naked. She didn't deserve privacy now, she thought. She'd let anyone into her home, to her search—they could read Abigail's juvenile journals, see her worst double-chin photographs and bad housekeeping, her favorite ratty underwear, if her daughter came back.

She knew things were missing from the closet—she'd been in that closet so many times, hide-and-seek, arranging and rearranging the dresses-to-grow-into, then a lull, then searching for any sort of evidence after she found the drugs.

But she couldn't remember what else belonged, what else was missing; her mental catalog was a mess. The prom dress, the champagne silk; she went with Timmy of course, lost in their collective happiness—where was it? Yes. Here was the narrow lavender sheath she'd worn to graduation. A lipstick stain on the collar, dirt on the hem. The dress was more beautiful; Linsey had been less beautiful in it because she was miserable about Timmy, but pretended the breakup had been her own idea. An appeasement for Abigail—but a lie.

Linsey had all the silver half-dollars Abigail had left for her, as the tooth fairy, in one of Joe's old socks with the leg end tied. It looked like a weapon. Where was her daughter? Abigail thought about the three days before she went missing, as the detective had suggested, looking at a calendar, writing out her hours, remembered what she had been doing. Nothing important. It was shocking to see her days written out like that, how much time she frittered away looking out windows or driving to soccer practice or holding on to cooking magazines without reading, as if they might emit some great source of inspiration through contact with their glossy covers. What a waste, she thought, leaving her single-minded obsession with her daughter for a minute. What was she doing, was she living, or just ticking, a clock, winding down, using up its battery?

She wrote it down—she'd been chatting with Beth Boris, whom she had met in a Pilates class. Beth was one of those women who belonged here, who was comfortable in the snail shell of the town. They'd gossiped about other people's children and where they were accepted to college or wait-listed and Abigail had felt culpable by association but had nodded when Beth told her about the parties some kids had, drinking and sex on the lawns. She nodded and looked shocked when Beth told her their pediatrician's daughter was caught with hash and a pipe.

But at least Beth talked to her. Other neighbors nodded and said, "Let's get together!" and didn't mean it.

"Mom?" she said, into the phone, though *of course* it was her mother; her mother answered the phone with her same hello. A vocal mirror.

"Abby," said her mother, the only one who called her Abby. "How is my girl?"

"She's missing, Mom. I mean, she went somewhere, and we don't know where, or something happened—"

"I meant you," said her mother. "I assume you mean my granddaughter."

"Yes," said Abigail. "And I didn't mean to sound hysterical—"

"You didn't sound hysterical," said her mother. Something was clicking on her end. Was it knitting needles? Was she surfing the Web while they talked?

"But this is indeed a problem. I assume you've contacted all her friends?"

"All her friends," said Abigail. "And the police."

"Oh, my. What about the boyfriend—Timothy?"

"Her ex. He doesn't know. We have a private detective." It

felt like failure, like confession. Why was she always the one with problems?

"Well, she's not that impetuous. Have you called the boy's college? What is it—University of Oregon?"

"California."

"You do that," said her mother. "How are the boys? Do you need me there?"

Yes, Abigail thought. *Yes, yes, yes.* But her mother was old, and needed more care than she gave, at last. Suddenly old, too. It had been six years since her father died, and for the first four, her mother was a seventy-something adventurer, free to go on senior tours of Europe and to learn new things; she took Investing Online at the library, she did genealogical research for herself and her friends, she learned orchid breeding but decided it was too expensive and besides, she wanted to be free to come and go, without heeding the whims and needs of flowers. She went on tours of China, Brazil, with her friends. She took tango lessons with mostly women in the class. Mardi Gras—something Abigail could hardly imagine: bare breasts, beads, bourbon, her turtleneck-prudish mother. Then she had a mild stroke—Abigail had gone to stay with her for two weeks, Linsey had come for a few days, too, better at tending than Abigail, more patient with bedpans and circular conversations—and now Abigail's mother was an old person. She sold the house and moved to an assisted-living facility.

"No, Mom, but thank you."

"Find the boy," she said.

Find the boy, Abigail thought. Ask the boy over and pretend I wasn't hateful to him. She walked upstairs to Linsey's room again, her legs heavy. When had stairs become such an effort? She ran her fingers through Linsey's clothing in the closet, looked inside her shoes. She found a bracelet she thought she'd lost inside an old boat shoe, something Linsey hadn't worn since junior high school, perhaps. Turquoise and silver beads. Joe had bought the bracelet for her in New Mexico, on their last trip together, before the divorce. She'd felt like an invalid there; Joe was doing research for a photo essay he was trying to place with *Car and Driver*—he was out most mornings in the rented Mustang (only silver was available instead of the red Joe had hoped for, and Abigail thought he might cry at the rental agency) taking preliminaries of rural routes. She lay in bed in the hotel suite, thinking about how much money was ticking away with each hour in that room, the rented spaces and the car, the babysitter she'd hired to help her mother with Linsey, since her mother's back had been bothering her and Linsey required chasing. Since she didn't trust anyone with Linsey, not really, not even her mother. Her stomach hurt every day on that trip, and when she and Joe made love, every evening, after too much food at another Zagat-rated restaurant, too much red wine and chocolate flourless desserts that tasted like soil to Abigail, it felt like a horrible sort of work. Still, when Joe gave her the bracelet on the plane on the way home, she had felt a tiny flower of hope opening in her chest. She knew it was probably just because they were going home, but she'd kissed him, and his mouth was soft enough against hers, for once, and when the bracelet disappeared she mourned it just a little. She fingered the smooth silver beads, then put it in Linsey's trunk instead of back into the shoe. If her daughter was going to steal her things, let her know her mother would notice. But she could have it, she could have the bracelet, she could have all her jewelry, she could have her emerald engagement ring from Frank, she could have her car and her refrigerator and her journals and her letters from her father, if only Linsey would come home.

She checked in with Barq again, and then the police. It was like swallowing bitter pain pills.

"Providence isn't panning out. Nothing even happened with this guy—it was just her friend's idea, the picture. I'm coming back to your neighborhood, but you may get the best intel there if you talk to all your neighbors. Oh, and I've got an agent tracking your boyfriend now," Barq said. His voice like his name. "God bless."

"Thanks for checking in, ma'am," said the police detective assigned to them, Martin Wooster. She didn't like his eyebrows, they looked plucked. She tried to listen to him, picking at her cuticles, it hurt, but he never said anything. "Don't forget, the best tips come from gossip, from door-to-door. We'll keep you posted, though."

Posted on what? The lunch on his desk? Who took this kind of job? Who could eat lunch when daughters were missing?

Door-to-door. She felt like a Girl Scout, selling cookies, with her clipboard with three questions, so she wouldn't forget, only instead of a uniform, she wore khakis, a button-down blouse. Still formal, still awkward. The detective had suggested she should keep things light with the neighbors, that they'd be more helpful if they were less worried, that worried people closed up, snap, he'd clapped his hands into a clam. But she didn't want to wear a dress, too feminine, she didn't want to wear jeans, too casual, too unconcerned. She thought of all the famous cases of murder within a family; wondered if anyone wondered about her. Would she, would she think her neighbors capable of the worst kinds of things? Could she suspect any of her neighbors of hurting Linsey? Her town had its history—two or three teen suicides; a mother, down the street, who killed herself with her policeman husband's handgun, suffering from postpartum depression—this was during Abigail's year of the bed, she hardly knew anything about it, just that it took ages for the house to sell. And it hadn't seemed real to her—the case against the football players who molested a retarded girl two towns over. There were blue ribbons on the houses of the people who thought the boys were innocent, yellow ribbons on those who believed the girl had been abused. It was strangely political, all these personal and private tortures.

3 CEDAR COURT

He was looking at her photos again—looking for clues in Linsey's expression at a birthday party last year, the twins', to which Geo had not been invited, but which he'd observed over the fence. He wanted to be on the other side of the fence—not that he minded his own home, not that he didn't have enough people here, but he always felt that he could belong over there, too, with Toby, anyway, with the stepfather, with Linsey herself, who understood being part of and being different.

He wouldn't tell anyone this, because it would sound creepy. He wasn't creepy. Linsey was laughing as a blindfolded Cody swung a bat at a piñata shaped like a football. Really they were already too old for piñatas last year, but Cody clearly enjoyed the destruction, the impact.

Geo preferred to put things together.

In one shot the candy was a shower landing on the lawn, pink and red wrapper rain. Linsey's mouth was open with words or joy, Geo wasn't sure which. He sorted through another stack. Linsey was leaving the house. Linsey was in the crowd at the Fourth of July, a shock of bright hair and smooth light skin—you'd think he'd been watching her, but really, he had photographs of all his neighbors. Circumstance; her bubble beside his bubble.

Maybe she ran away; it made sense for the first time to Geo. There were no menacing men in a single photograph— and she was hardly ever with anyone other than her family and Timmy. Of course, she had whole sections of life he could never record, but he could see how she might feel missing within this very concrete one—the girl whose father no longer lived in the house.

He wondered whether she loved her stepfather. He was so steady, such a tripod of a man. In a way, Geo wished his own father was more like that, thicker, less vulnerable. He looked at Linsey on Timmy's shoulders at that same Fourth of July. They were both wearing blue shirts and red bandannas. She was tall enough that she looked like she'd topple them both. If she didn't have Timmy, who did she have here? Of course, she was about to go to college. About to leave anyway. He stared into the laughing photo face. She had something under her arm—a notebook. If he looked hard enough, maybe he could see inside.

Downstairs, wondering whether Timmy might stop by again, Geo fidgeted with the sea beans in the mancala board—gifts from his well-traveled uncle. The sea beans came from Florida, but they fit in the African game board, sliding smooth between his fingers; he wanted two in each little cup, but there weren't enough. It hurt him a little, the imbalance, one omitted from a cup on each side. He picked at the place where the stems once attached.

His mother hadn't noticed the bruise on his neck, a good, hearty purple already, which would evolve into the strange maroon specific to Geo's bruises, when he bruised, which he only did when he fell or something struck him very hard, something sharp enough, swung with force, but not so sharp as to cut him, to spill his blood, to break him. Geo hated bruises, but his mother hated them more; she always checked them hourly, like a broody hen examines her eggs.

He'd been caught up in thinking about the Stein family—about Linsey, about how they needed help and maybe he could do something, maybe there was something in his photographs, or something he'd seen and hadn't remembered. He didn't think it could happen so quickly with Cody Stein. He'd always worried about Cody, who never bullied him in school, never directly, but who always looked at him nervously. Cody's best friend Banks said things about Oreos and pretended Geo was a basketball player. Geo was terrible at basketball. When Cody and Geo were paired up to complete electrical circuits in science, Cody had tried to zap himself with the wires, and Geo had stopped him, his own hands over Cody's, not sure why, maybe because it seemed like a waste of electricity, maybe because his father stopped others' pain whenever he could. Cody had peeped, "Hey!" but not much else, and they'd finished their circuit together, saying almost nothing.

This time he could've avoided the whole business with Cody, only he didn't want to leave his own backyard just because his neighbor threw a football over the fence. He didn't want to throw it back, either, which was all Cody had asked. His neighbor was playing with Banks, whose mother dropped him off at school in a red Jaguar. She wore gloss-slick lipstick to match the car and blew kisses like an aging movie star.

Maybe Cody was especially nervous about Linsey disappearing. From what Geo had learned about boys, sometimes fear turned to anger, and sometimes fear turned to a sort of paralysis. He wasn't sure he'd ever seen his father afraid, and he wasn't sure he ever wanted to. But boys, they were often afraid.

The article about Linsey had just been in the *Ridgewood Times* today, and the kids at school were talking about reporters from the *Bergen Record* who interviewed people right in town in front of the post office as if there'd been something civic happening, instead of a private disturbance. The headline in the local paper said "Family Desperate for Leads." Her high school yearbook photo, a family photo, Linsey squeezing one half brother on each side. Timmy had been texting him for the past few days, and he'd stopped by the house, and talked to him like he was a much older kid. Respectful. He gave Timmy a scanned copy of the photo collage of Linsey; they'd watched it print out slowly on glossy paper Geo had gotten for his birthday from his great-aunt, sheet by sheet he used it, and the expensive ink, a good print.

The ball had bounced twice before it landed in his mother's hosta. Geo liked the shape of a football, such a strange turd of a ball, those pointed ends and all the weight in the middle. He played touch football sometimes with his uncle Dan, his mother's brother, who let him ride on his shoulders still, so Geo felt tall and relaxed around Uncle Dan. He threw well, his uncle said, and he ran well, just not at the same time.

"Dude, I know you're back there making your weird art project," Cody called over the fence.

He hadn't needed to say *weird*. Geo wasn't setting bottle caps, anyway, he was just cleaning them, with cotton balls and rubbing alcohol from his sisters' bathroom. He had pilfered a bottle of clear nail polish, too; he was thinking about lacquering the tops of the whole lot of them, to keep them a little cleaner, to keep them from rusting.

"Dude! Throw the ball back, okay?" Cody yelled. He could see his neighbor's blue Giants tank top through the slats of the fence. Slices of his skinny arms. He felt a shock of something, loss, perhaps—he almost wanted to comfort the boy. His sister, she was missing.

Geo didn't say anything. He was working on a Sam Adams Winter Wheat. There was no dent at all in the cap, but it didn't look like a twist off. He liked the smell of beer.

"Dude!" Cody yelled again.

"Just climb over, dude," Banks instructed his friend.

When he was little, he could forget he was black from time to time. Most of the faces he looked at were white, though Minal's wasn't; most of his world was the same as theirs. Except for the distance. Everyone kept a distance from him. Ordinary people, those who didn't know him, that is. The teacher touched him, a bit too much. The gym teacher patted his back and gave him high-fives, the same way, only he noticed then, the contrast in the colors of their hands. But on the sidewalk, people spread around him when he walked. Especially now that he was older, it was as though he walked inside parentheses, keeping him from the other words of the sentence, just a bit off from everyone else. He knew the store detectives followed him in Lord & Taylor when he went with his mother for a blue blazer for his sister's graduation. He knew they watched him in the bug-eye mirror at CVS, keeping tabs on the whereabouts of his hands. He knew people expected just a little less of him, and just a little more.

"There's the fucking ball," said Banks. They had both jumped the fence. It wasn't that high, four feet at the point of the highest slat on the curve, but somehow, Geo had thought of it as impenetrable. He had wanted them to be too discouraged to bother him anymore. He had wanted to keep Cody's angry sorrow at a distance.

"Why the fuck didn't you just throw it back?" Banks was approaching him now, holding the football and a clump of white-and-green-striped hosta leaves. His mother loved her hosta. She called it her "hostile," but she was proud of its yearly expansion.

"Busy," said Geo, glaring at the leaves. He could smell their ruined green. How did Linsey have a brother like this? She might have gone to parties, like it said in the paper, she might have been drunk from time to time, but she wasn't spiteful or small; he knew from the way she looked in photographs.

"Dude, your neighbor is a prick," Banks said to Cody, who was loitering by the fence, scrutinizing Geo with his bottle caps, a look of transfixed disgust on his face, as if Geo were dissecting a squirrel, slicing a live worm. Cody gripped a broken chunk of the fence in his hand, the fence from Geo's side, the triangle point up like a flame.

"I was busy," said Geo. "You have your ball."

"*You have your ball,*" mimicked Banks. He kicked at Cody, differed contempt.

"Fuck you," said Cody, but as Banks climbed back over to the Steins', Cody walked over to Geo. He reached for the bottle cap in Geo's hand.

"That's mine," said Geo, withdrawing, a cotton ball in his fist, the alcohol evaporating, chilling his palm. He didn't know what he expected next. His heart wasn't warning him, the way it usually did when someone was planning to hurt him, a kicking from within.

"Stupid kid," said Cody, apparently so annoyed that he'd swiped air, so infuriated that Geo hadn't stopped his work to help them, so appalled by Banks's kick, that he had to hurt Geo. His mouth was horrible, a thin, straight line, but new pink, bud pink, worm pink. He pressed those thin lips together and dug his toe under the bottle cap mosaic, scattered Geo's work with three sharp punts.

Geo wanted to go over the fence, sometimes, but he didn't want them to come over to his side.

"Cut it out!" Geo grabbed Cody's back to stop him, keeping clear of the feet, but then Cody turned and struck him, hard, in the neck, with the broken fence slat he still gripped in his hand.

"What's this?" Geo's mother asked, as Geo put the Mancala board away. She was drying her hands—she'd been cooking something and her hands smelled of torn greens. Geo stiffened, his neck hurt, he could feel the bruise through the collar of his polo shirt. He'd changed upstairs, buttoned up. He'd washed his alcohol-dry hands of dust. No blood on the surface, just pooling under the skin. He felt burned, raw to the air. His mother held up the note he'd found in the backyard a few days ago, the folded paper, water-stained then, only now it was just a linty mass from the laundry.

Geo sighed. He didn't have many secrets from his mother, just the ones that hurt her more than him. She'd seen the Linsey collage—they'd given it to the detective, too, another good print. She had real and artificial smiles. Geo felt almost possessive of her temporary joys, her unedited expressions. She had to be okay. It would ruin too many people's lives if she wasn't.

"That's something I found in the backyard. I couldn't read it. I don't know the writing."

Geo knew handwriting. He knew his father's, which was almost as bad as a doctor's: a backward, lefty's scrawl. His mother wrote in stunning block letters, like an artist, the letters more about shape and space than instruction. She'd tried to teach him calligraphy last summer; they'd assembled on the front porch in the slant green light of July. She shaped his name on a thick rectangle of clean white. He'd practiced; she'd given him his own Japanese brush and a smooth gray stone. Geo tried to compose lines as sure as hers, but he *wasn't* as sure; he couldn't bear letters that didn't hold up their own houses, sloppy lines, so he had decided to wait until his fingers were more confident. He hadn't told her that. He told her he'd lost his stone.

Geo knew which sister had left an unsigned note on the kitchen table from the writing. He knew Cody's and Toby's lettering, from sitting in seats close to theirs in school. They were *S* and *W,* alphabetical neighbors. These were the things he noticed, it wasn't his fault. He knew Cody bit his nails and that the dots he made for the lowercase *i* and exclamation points were little bubbles holding nothing. He knew Cody peeled off scabs. He knew Cody hadn't actually meant to hit him.

"Do you think—maybe? Do you think this note could've come from next door? Do you think?"

He hadn't been thinking about it at all when he pocketed the paper. He knew Linsey Hart was missing. He'd been the one to unfold the first flyer when it came in the mail slot a few days ago. He'd found himself wondering what the twins knew, wondering whether they missed their sister, whether they loved her the way he loved his sisters, like limbs, like body parts you expect to do their work without instruction, part of your whole. Linsey's weren't whole siblings, though, just halves. That made them more different than he was from his sisters; they shared full blood. Victoria, with her red wavy hair, had the whitest skin he'd seen, almost blue. You could see veins through her skin. She also had eyes shaped like his, and her hands matched his, and her knees turned in a little, the way his did.

The newspaper said the whole family was in shock. It said Toby and Cody were close as can be to their half sister. He wondered why they bothered with pointing out half, if they were that close, who needed the distance of details? If one of his sisters disappeared, Geo would look for her. He wouldn't play in the backyard. He wouldn't get angry, but he would be really scared. He needed his sister, and he needed Linsey to come back, the way he needed to hear the final note of a song. Maybe he could help.

"It could be," he said to his mother. And it could. It could be something. It could be evidence. It could also be the last of Linsey's high school homework, it could be Mrs. Sentry's note to her house cleaner, it could be from blocks away. He was touching his collar, an involuntary protection.

"I could take it over to them?" his mother said. Geo thought for a minute.

"Maybe we should call the police," he mumbled.

"You think—hey, what is that? Why are you so dressed up? Geo?" His mother put her hand over his. She possessed him in the way only his mother could, and she pulled his fingers and collar back to reveal the damage. Then she gasped, as if she'd seen the blow.

26 SYCAMORE STREET

Everyone knew, of course, there was nothing casual about the signs Frank had made and stapled to poles all over town. Linsey in her graduation attire, her grin slightly lopsided— she'd hated that photo, though Abigail thought it was perfect, showing ambivalence. Ambivalently, she went to the next house, and the next. She spoke to open faces—have you seen my daughter, Linsey, recently? Have you heard anything about her? Have you heard any rumors or anything unusual or have you seen anything suspect in the neighborhood? *Anything suspect* was the code for suspicious people. Mexican lawn workers, the black mail carrier when he was new. She hated that—*she* didn't mean that. The first person she spoke with, a new neighbor she hardly knew, said, no, no, no, sorry. That was it. The second offered her cookies. She couldn't eat cookies. She couldn't eat anything, but she accepted one anyway, a lopsided chocolate chip, and slid it into her sleeve instead of biting. The next house held a fight so loud she hesitated, but rang anyway. The man who was screaming stopped, answering the door. Mr. Corning, a lawyer. His face was fat with anger, his eyes bright. Was he crying?

"May I help you?"

"I'm sorry to intrude, but—"

"Oh, no, no problem," he said. He was playing with something in his pocket. Change? A pocketknife?

"I was wondering if you've seen my daughter, Linsey Hart?" She held up her poster.

"This is NOT A GOOD TIME!" screamed Mrs. Corning from the other room.

"I'm sorry, I'll go," said Abigail.

"No," said Mr. Corning. He reached out and grabbed her arm, a quick grip. It hurt all the way to the bone.

"GO AWAY!" screamed Mrs. Corning.

"I'm sorry," said Abigail. Mr. Corning had already retreated, patting her before pulling his arm away, incongruously gentle.

At Reeva Sentry's house, she had only just rung when the door swung wide open and Reeva, her mouth a slick plum, opened the screen and extended her hand. She touched Abigail's arm, and Abigail thought she might start sobbing, but this was not why she'd come. She and Reeva were never friends—Reeva had offered her some hand-me-downs from her boys for Abigail's boys, and Abigail had taken them all, afraid to offend by sorting through the six bags of beautifully folded navy blazers, long shorts, T-shirts with skateboard decals. Worn elastics, occasional grass stains, but expensive things, well made. She had donated most of the stash, because

Frank liked buying clothes for the boys. He took them to out-let stores on long weekends and braved the crowds and some-how the boys came home proud of their purchases, taking off the tags by themselves before putting the turtlenecks, polo shirts, thick cotton sweaters into the wash unasked. She sus-pected he bribed them with computer games or even cash, which was not entirely a bad idea.

"Oh, Mrs. Stein, come on in—," said Reeva, wearing what Abigail could only think of as a hospital face, the expression you offer your great-aunt when she's septic and smells of plastic IV tubing.

"That's okay," said Abigail, trying to stand her ground on the stoop, but Reeva tugged at her.

Abigail watched Reeva's face as she stepped in the door, thinking how Reeva had trusted Linsey, how Reeva had hired Linsey, how Linsey had relationships in this world she couldn't even imagine. The detective had asked about her laptop and her phone and was reviewing texts, and he had downloaded some files from the computer at the desk in the family room. Toby and Cody were angry with both mother and daughter: "He can see what I wrote to MY friends," Toby said. "And he can see all my scores on my games," Cody said. "That's so unfair." But she knew they just felt strange the way they did. Her own messages were on that computer—messages to Frank at work; love notes; messages to the college friends she never spoke with on the phone anymore; messages to her friend Mel, whom she had sort of dated between marriages, about whom she had never been serious, but with whom sex had been thrilling—she didn't know which messages the detective might be reading, and despite knowing she had to give everything up for her daughter, she resented that intrusion.

"You need tea or coffee?" said Reeva. She wore gold eye shadow; it made her eyes seem very dark, but it was lovely, Abigail thought, lovely in that way she would never attain, lovely as in put together. She didn't need to be put together. She needed her family together, that was all. "Or something else? I'll put on whatever you'd like."

"That's all right," said Abigail. "I just wanted to ask—"

"I wanted to tell you," said Reeva, parking Abigail at her kitchen table and turning toward the electric chrome kettle on the counter. She had one of those instant hot water taps, something Frank wanted to get as soon as the boys were old enough not to mess with it—probably when they were twenty-four, Abigail had said—but she filled the kettle with water from a filter pitcher in the fridge. Cold to hot, thought Abigail.

"I wanted to mention, I mean, I saw something you might want to know about—"

"Did you see Linsey? What?" Abigail stood up.

"It's not *that* good, honey," said Reeva, touching her again, hand on her shoulder: sit.

"I just noticed, well, I saw that Mr. Leonard when I was on a walk, I mean I was in the neighborhood, you know, near the Hopsmiths'?—I was on my way to a book group? You have one of those at the temple, don't you?"

Abigail nodded, though she didn't have any book group at the temple. She only really went to the temple on high holy days. It was just for Frank, it was her hypocritical indulgence. Maybe this was what had angered God; maybe she should go to confession.

"And I saw that Mr. Leonard, on a walk in the woods? And anyway, he had this pink sweatshirt? It looked a lot like one of hers; I know, because she babysat for me?"

"Oh. Thank you," said Abigail, writing it down. Mr. Leonard? Mr. Leonard who saw them through the windows? Who sometimes waved, as if they were passing on a train? Mr. Leonard with his music early in the morning? Linsey had been to his house over the years. She'd sold him Girl Scout cookies; she'd walked his dog. Mr. Leonard had her sweatshirt? She imagined it, Mr. Leonard's thin arm raised to strike Linsey. Couldn't be, couldn't be, still, she reached for her cell phone—she was going to call Barq first, then the police.

"It's just that he's rather an odd man, and he's right next door to you—you know— Do you have any news at all?"

The sweatshirt. She caught herself, she was breathing fast, almost panting, dialing the phone without looking at Reeva. She didn't press Send, not yet.

"Are you sure it was her sweatshirt?"

"Well, it looked like it, but I wasn't that close—I was, um, just passing by the Hopsmiths'. It could've been someone else's, you know, the pink ones from the girls' swim team?"

Abigail paused in her dialing. She knew that sweatshirt.

She thought they'd packed it in the trunk, but then, she hadn't seen it for a while. For a few weeks at least. She looked at Reeva, who was still chattering, her mouth open, a fish, Abigail thought. She'd call it in, of course, but what was it really—just a rumor?

"And of course I called the police—"

"Pardon?" asked Abigail.

"I assumed you knew, because I called the police about it. Yesterday."

Nothing, they told her nothing. She envisioned Martin Wooster, tipping back his chair at his big metal desk, eating a sandwich, writing "sweatshirt" on a pad. Then letting mustard spot the note. No, he wasn't incompetent. She was just desperate.

"Oh, so you already called about it? Oh. They didn't tell me—"

"Hmm. I'm surprised they didn't tell you. I walk near that woods spot quite a lot. I even saw Linsey there—"

"You SAW Linsey?"

"Oh, honey, early this summer. She took my Johnny for a woods walk. She's a good girl, isn't she?"

Something in her tone told Abigail she was asking, not being rhetorical. Always them, she thought, and us. But Reeva was here for her now—maybe there was something about this queen bee she could rely on. Or maybe she was just being lulled by the honey and the wing beats.

"Yes," said Abigail. "You have a daughter? Nina?"

"Tina is much younger than Linsey. Just a freshman." She

seemed to reconsider after she said this. "I guess that's not all that much younger."

"You are changing diapers and then you are applying to college. It's that fast."

Reeva laughed, almost honestly. "Is Linsey still seeing that Timmy? He was such an athlete. I hear his house is up for sale. Someone said some people had already put in an offer. Maybe they were *Korean*?" She whispered this last word. Hissed it. "Do you know? I don't mind Japanese, but the Koreans always keep to themselves—"

"No. I mean, they broke up. I don't know who's buying the house. People, just people." Abigail looked at her clipboard. She was going to call now.

"Oh, that's hard, first love. Have you asked him if he knows anything?"

"He's moving to California," she said, thinking, *I have to GO.*

"Oh, and have you checked with his parents?"

"Thank you, Reeva," said Abigail, getting up.

"Oh," said Reeva. "Glad to be of help."

Now Abigail felt nauseated, the smell of the chocolate apricots lingering in her nose. *She's a good girl, isn't she? They always keep to themselves.* Why must there always be an *other*? She was just as *other* in her acquired Jewishness. She didn't like Reeva Sentry. Gossipmonger. Sure, she'd been hospitable, but she probably inspected all the neighbors' recycling to find out who drank cheap wine and who ate frozen entrees. Abigail felt guilty for thinking it—Reeva had not been unkind, just chattery. She had said something about the sweatshirt; no one else had contributed a thing. It was noticing something; it was paying attention.

On the sidewalk, she dialed Barq's number. She got voice mail. "Do you know about the sweatshirt?" she asked. "Did you know Reeva Sentry saw Mr. Leonard with a sweatshirt that looked like Linsey's? Is that something? She said she called Wooster—or the cops, anyway—call me."

Then the police. Martin Wooster was at his desk. *Why aren't you out finding my daughter?* "Did you get a call about a sweatshirt?" she asked.

"Oh, yes, hello, Mrs. Stein." He took much too long to breathe.

"We did. We investigated. It was a dead lead, so we didn't want to get you overexcited."

"A dead lead?"

"Your neighbor buried a bird in a pink handkerchief. Somehow someone thought he had Linsey's shirt. He didn't."

"Oh," said Abigail. "Are you sure?"

"Sure," said Martin Wooster.

He mumbled something like be in touch and was already gone as Abigail was apologizing, explaining.

A dead lead. A dead bird.

She made her way down the cul-de-sac, her chest compressed. A dead lead. Maybe someone had a live lead, electrical, a current to jolt this cold hunt to life. She rang at three houses with no answer, then the Whitebreads. She hardly knew them now, but when she'd moved in, Mrs. Whitebread,

Jane, had brought her banana bread and a jar of honey with a plaid ribbon. She'd sat on the front step with Jane, beginning the process of friend making. But somehow they never became friends, even though their boys saw each other at school, somehow they had children and built the hives of their families and woes in their separate lots and only waved half the time their cars passed.

"Mrs. Whitebread?" she asked, when Jane answered the door.

"Abigail," said Jane. "I heard about Linsey, I'm so sorry." She reached her arm around Abigail and ushered her into the room. Her son was on the floor, playing the game where you scooped rocks along a board—an African game of some kind, she thought, blushing, because the son was black. He looked up at her, and she thought he narrowed his eyes, making him feline, long lashed, angry. That was awful, how could she think he was angry? She smiled at him, but his glance was already cast back at the game.

She'd heard rumors that he was the result of a mix-up with the markings on sperm donations, and also that Mrs. Whitebread had had a black lover, but she didn't believe the latter, and the former, well, that was their business. Maybe he was adopted. Who cared? She wanted to like the son, though she didn't remember his name. He played at the back of the yard, near theirs, making little nests with detritus from the recycling bins. Toby said he was always making movies and taking photographs. He was so quiet, sometimes she wondered if something was wrong with him. She also wondered why her sons didn't befriend him, if perhaps they should, if she should encourage them, but she let them be when it came to friends, caring mostly about safety and car pools to soccer.

Jane sat on the couch beside a nest of laundry. The basket was on the floor. She gestured that Abigail should sit down on the chair, but Abigail was afraid to settle anywhere. She asked her questions.

"No," said Jane. "I haven't heard anything. I did know your daughter's boyfriend—Timmy? He volunteered a few years ago for this little drama class Geo was in? He was a nice young man."

What odd words, thought Abigail, coming from someone so much more colorful than *nice young man*.

"They broke up."

"Oh, I'm sorry," said Jane. She began to fold the laundry, her daughter's long-limbed fall T-shirts, Geo's socks; she was trying to match the shades of white before she paired them from the masses.

"Any rumors, perhaps, in town?"

"Hmm. Well, I have to admit, I did see some kids looking at one of the posters—" She glanced at her son, and without looking up at her, he left the room. Abigail listened to his heavy steps up the uncarpeted staircase. A door sighed open and whined shut.

"I heard someone saying something about drugs, Abigail. I feel horrible telling you this, but it was something about you catching your daughter with pot—I'm so sorry—I feel awful saying it—"

"No, that's okay, this was something we went through—it wasn't a big deal, though at first I thought it was." She shivered, though the windows were open and the afternoon was warm. She felt naked there, spilling out the contents of her house, of her family history, for this woman she hardly knew. "But thank you for telling me. Who was talking about it?"

"Some teenager, and some young man who works at Starbucks? I think he lives in the carriage house behind the Hopsmiths'. They didn't say her name, just gestured toward the poster? Is there anything I can do to help?"

"Just let me know if you hear anything else," said Abigail, moving slowly toward the door. Her daughter's face was all over town, and her daughter's business was all over town, and her daughter was missing, wasn't this enough? Couldn't she just come home now? Abigail looked through the window—she could see the fence and her own backyard from here. Frank's car was pulling in. Maybe she should leave.

"I will, I will," said Jane. She was worrying a linty piece of folded paper from the laundry in her hand.

Abigail didn't know the contents of these houses. She knew their faces: brick and mortar, lights on the flanks of the red front doors, aluminum siding, stained wood, one a yellow as pale as a goldfinch's belly feather, she'd seen it painted three times since she'd lived there, the trucks and ladders; the tarps; and the sharp, sour paint smell as she'd driven past with her windows open.

The cell phone rang, and Abigail leapt off the sidewalk, lifting with adrenaline.

"Abby," said Margaret. "I have a new list of possibilities for you. And I have this amazing new crème from Shiseido—how are you, babe?"

"I'm—" She stood, unable to say it. *Looking for my lost daughter. A wreck. Help.* "Okay," she finished.

"You'll be better once you start brainstorming with me. Cupcake Café is looking for kitchen prep help—I know that's really not your thing, and it wouldn't be for long. Probably would cost more than it brings in given the commute but, honey, you could learn so much for your own café. What do you think of cupcakes?"

"I . . . I don't think cupcakes are right?" *I'm going door-to-door asking for leads. My Linsey is missing.* If she told Margaret, it would be too real to bear. She should. She couldn't.

"Okay, don't worry, some of this is closer to home. There's even real estate. I know that's a stretch for you, too—"

Abigail laughed, a fake laugh. "No way, not real estate, that's not me," she said, letting this be about her, letting herself be important to her friend. She was crying as quietly as she could.

"Okay, gotta go, but I'm e-mailing you this list. Don't pooh-pooh everything, open mind, my dear, open mind."

"Okay."

"Are you okay? You sound stressed?" Margaret had to go, she would let her go. It would be in all the papers soon, and then there'd be no choice but to talk with everyone

about it. All the time. Until Linsey came home. And probably after.

Margaret signed off and Abigail tried to swallow the
lump in her throat. It was like lying, but she couldn't tell her
friend that Linsey was gone. Then Abigail stared at her phone
again, wondering whether Linsey had ever really talked with
Margaret, whether she would have confided—no, Margaret
couldn't be so blithe if she knew anything. It was awful—
everyone suddenly seemed suspicious. Abigail was walking,
faster and faster, feeling her body move, the muscles stretched
with unaccustomed effort. How long had it been since she
abandoned her car, how long had it been since she'd walked
long and far in this neighborhood, past the houses she knew,
into the storybook realm of unknown neighbors' lives? The
last time she remembered walking here, it was with the baby,
one week old, and Linsey, just four. She'd let her daughter
push the stroller; the baby had been hard asleep, his eyes
winched shut against the world. It had been summer, late
summer, like this, and she'd never expected what had come
next, only had watched her daughter peel a Band-Aid off her
finger and tighten her mouth in concentration as she pushed
the carriage, a heavy thing from Joe's mother, with shock-
absorbing springs and its own mattress. Linsey had to reach
overhead to grip the bar.

She jogged down the path into the woods, as if she might
find something there. The trees stood like sentries on the riv-
erbank, and she walked faster, faster, peering into the water.
They should drag the river, she thought, horrifying herself by

imagining her daughter's bloated face, a severed limb. No, no, no. There was occasional litter on the path, a half-flattened beer can, the glitter of crushed glass. A flyer for a new Japanese restaurant in town. A note about band practice. But mostly, just the lobed leaves of jewelweed, shiny poison ivy swaddling the shrubbery, oaks and maples and sycamores casting long shadows across the path. What did she expect to find in here, she wondered—a tree house, a shack, a secret tunnel? Three times she'd come down here, looking in the little strip of woods. Once alone, once with her husband, once with Barq, who kicked over stones as if her daughter might be hiding with pill bugs and earthworms. She had read that more than half of runaways stay close to home, that some abducted teens were held within a mile of the place from which they'd been taken.

Abigail stopped; someone was coming. Her heart kept up its work, though she wasn't breathing. Then an elderly man passed, his basset hound on a leash, his ears pink and his cheeks bristly, her ears dragging the path like a net. The path ended, and Abigail was back on the street in the gloaming. She started running. Her legs felt good, that ache. The leaves leaving the early maples, yellowed, with green still gripping their veins, tumbled into the street. It was windy now, as if the ending day was full of breath. The leaves ran away from her, fast down the street, and then Abigail was running, too, stretching her legs long, remembering what it felt like to be a dancer in high school—her mother had wanted her to be a dancer, had sat through lessons when mothers were long since gone during the instruction, had hoped for Clara in the annual *Nutcracker,* though Abigail was once the nutcracker itself, because she was limber, fast, could jump high, and was never going to be tall. She had a good body for comedy, her teacher had said. Not drama. Why hadn't God listened to that? Where was the comedy in her life right now? Only Frank, only her husband, who joked about the detective's funny eyebrows to keep her from weeping. She was running hard now, and had left the sidewalk for the street, running past the turnoff for town, toward the reservoir path, wearing her sensible, nonthreatening clothes for interviewing neighbors. The blouse buttons strained as she swayed her arms, her khakis were ridiculous for running, but she had to keep going. On the path, she passed a man from her neighborhood, Reeva's husband, Mr. Sentry. He looked at her, the quick passing-jogger glance, then nodded his head to the music attached to his ears. He wore embarrassing Lycra shorts and a tank top—tank tops on middle-aged men seemed like such a desperate thing, she thought, though Frank wore tank-top undershirts, but he'd never wear them around the backyard like a Jewish mafioso. He'd never jog, either, though just before they married he joined a gym for two months, worked out, and returned home wearing zipper-front sweatshirts and looking proud. He should work out, she realized, he needed to be in better shape if he was going to live long enough for her. Everyone left her, everyone. She took the cutoff from the reservoir, the one that linked to the Long Path, which linked to the rails-to-trails project that followed the highway up to the New York border. She kept running. Her legs burned and her lungs hurt. She couldn't stop, so she shoved the few notes from her clipboard in her pocket and threw away the board itself and the pen, childlike in her pride as she dunked them into a trash can without stopping. She would make it to New York, she would keep running, she would run through states and across the surface of lakes and into Canada and across oceans until she found her daughter. Then her leg cramped. A fist of muscle. She couldn't keep running. She stopped and leaned on a spindly birch limb, breathing and breathing, her lungs burning, rubbing her ridiculous calf.

She turned to hobble toward home. When she got there the mail would be in the box—and she would have to unfold the paper; she would have to see what everyone was about to learn of her family's private despair.

Timmy did not trust Jordan House, the boy who worked at Starbucks—who supposedly breezed through college with all sorts of wunderkind skills but now attended coffee and sugar addictions and denned up in a garage behind the Hopsmiths' house as if he had no use for all that education. It wasn't that Timmy was a snob—if people had different talents, different intellects, different ways of living, that was one thing, but this was a sort of fringe choice, a hanging on, an arrested development.

Timmy had observed Jordan eyeing Linsey at one of those parties the kids on Brook Street had, too much space and parents away, too much money and booze and drugs and all the kids who looked for entertainment in the bad behavior of others clustering like vultures to a kill. He had gone because Linsey begged him, but then he'd convinced her to leave. It was one thing to visit with friends when they were a little drunk, but this was beyond a little—kids passed out on the lawn, two eighth-graders having awkward sex in the hostas—he was disgusted that so many people had no respect for themselves. And Jordan had been sitting on the porch watching people come and go, his legs spread too broad on the step as he leaned back and observed. It wasn't adult, and it wasn't child, and he almost went up to kick the bastard for looking at Linsey, lascivious, but he wasn't like that, he didn't fight over imagined slights—at least not in real life.

Timmy was sitting in the Starbucks wishing he hadn't handed his money to Jordan. Jordan handed him, in return, his coffee and a flyer about Linsey.

"I know, dude," Timmy had said. "She is—she was my girlfriend." His mouth burned with acid.

"Sorry, kid," said Jordan, trying to smother Timmy's "dude" with condescension. He was too handsome, Jordan. He was suspect.

Timmy breathed deep. He breathed deep again. He was probably heaving with breath here in Starbucks, but he knew better than to trap himself in suspecting this guy. This guy was a looker, not a doer.

"Peace, man," he said, and went to sit down in the nasty blue velvet chairs that smelled of banana peel.

Timmy had walked toward Linsey's house this morning, but stopped when he saw a small crowd of people and six cars parked in front. He could face Abigail, but he couldn't face a whole army.

Timmy sat with a notepad and wrote down all the people he didn't trust—Jordan House, Markos, the boy from Brown, himself. He didn't trust himself. That was part of the breakup, in fact. He had wanted Linsey too much—wanted what their bodies did together—to see staying with her, together, apart, together, apart, without needing to fill the longings between, the empty space. And he'd rather be apart than be a cheater.

"Hey," said the kid—Geo. Timmy wasn't used to the flow of people during the summer—during the year you rarely saw teens out during the day on open campus periods. Elementary school kids were in school.

"Hey," said Timmy.

"I have some ideas," said Geo. "And pictures," as if they were continuing an ongoing conversation.

Geo pulled out a file folder. A mosaic of photos of Linsey. Timmy started looking right away—he knew this one, from graduation, he knew this one, from a Science Saturday, in fact, when she'd come to help out with the World's Largest Domino Topple attempt (they'd made it to 1,652 before the dominos splayed and stopped).

"Tell me," said Timmy.

"She could have gone to visit her dad."

"Good guess, but that's out. He wouldn't hide her—he wouldn't want to go to jail."

"Okay, so what about this?" Geo pointed to a photo in the cluster—Linsey on someone's shoulders. He couldn't recognize the shoulders, and the boy's head was out of the picture. Not Markos—someone in a leather jacket. Pretentious, Timmy thought, then he sighed. It wouldn't help anyone if he was paranoid.

Geo took out a notebook—one of those marbled hard-covered single-subject notebooks Timmy thought of as writing journals, since they'd had to keep them since third grade.

He wondered whether there would be anything good in Linsey's, though usually people didn't write anything too personal, since the teachers, while they promised not to share with others, sometimes pointed out something they thought was terrific, and even read one aloud to class, only it was an awful story about wearing your pants backward in the fifth-grade play and struggling not to cry. He'd had some amazing teachers; he'd also had some bullies disguised as teachers. Timmy was awed when he'd gone along to see Linsey teach the kids in Paterson, respecting people regardless of age or ability. It was something his parents admired, too, and something innate, and probably why everyone thought she would become a teacher, for sure, though she'd told him she loved it but thought there might be more, other things she wanted to do.

"I'm still a kid," she'd said, leaning into his chest, making his fingers ache to take off her shirt. His body was a problem sometimes.

"So," said Geo. He'd been writing while Timmy thought about Linsey's body. "I've got the father, the music teacher, the guy from Brown—"

Timmy looked down and saw this list in bright blue Sharpie pen.

"I don't think any of those people is really suspect," said Timmy. "I get sick at the idea of anyone doing anything to her, but seriously, Geo, I think the main suspect you should have on that list is Linsey, just Linsey."

"Hmm," said Geo. "I appreciate that. But should I keep

going? I was planning to ask at the *Ridgewood Times* whether I could look through old photos and see if there's anything there."

"You're a good kid, Geo," said Timmy, though he was already feeling sick, knowing what he had to do.

"Look," said Geo. "There's something there." He pointed, obtusely, at the coffee counter, where Jordan the barista was leaning over toward a woman Timmy knew. Mrs. Sentry, he thought. He looked at Jordan's face, his hand over hers on the coffee cup.

"You're right," Timmy said, "there's something there." Linsey babysat for Mrs. Sentry. "Put them on the list," he said, sighing.

"I'll look for photos," Geo said. "I have a lot."

"No harm in looking," said Timmy, thinking maybe there was potential harm to cheaters and slimeballs. Helping, he was helping, but when you dig in the dirt, sometimes you find pill bugs, stinkbugs, worms, and bones.

Timmy and Geo walked back from town together; Geo pushed his bike and they shared a companionable silence for almost the entire mile. Timmy knew he had to tell Abigail that Linsey had secretly applied to Berkeley, Stanford, and Mills, considering transferring even though she'd always wanted to go to Cornell. The acceptance letters to Berkeley and Mills ("Stanford's too sunny anyway!" she said, crumpling their thin envelope) followed the portal lists and came to his house, because she'd wanted to keep this all to herself. For two weeks, she'd decided on Mills. "Think of all the women's studies!" she'd said. "I can learn to be a woman!" In a way, it had been funny, but in a way, it was true—college was that step forward, learning to live in the world.

The day they broke up she told him she was still going to Cornell, that her parents had paid the first tuition bill, griping as if they hadn't expected it—her mother, anyway. Her stepfather, she said, had told her, over poached breakfast eggs, *Please know you can call if you need anything, even money.* Timmy liked that guy. But maybe even he belonged on the list.

She'd said she wasn't considering Mills anymore, that she wasn't going to transfer, ever. But it occurred to him that she could have gone to visit—not to see him, but to see the other coast, to take in an alternative through her senses and not just pictures and ideas. He may have been the only person to know that she was far from sure about what she wanted to do when she grew up—everyone assumed she would be a teacher. Sure, maybe she'd get a Ph.D. in education, but that was where everyone thought her heart fit, her future. He knew Linsey wasn't sure about her future, about teaching, even about college—he knew she made a beautiful mask, but that she was insecure where other people thought she was sincerely smiling.

Geo wanted to help him—he could see something in that kid, a loop tape of Velcro looking for the hook side, a slipping up against the world that wanted purchase. Things had mostly been easy for Timmy, except for knowing, all his life, that he'd kept his parents from doing all the things they wanted to do, last child, last anchor. His older brother had spent two years with them in a slum in Peru; his sister had volunteered at the Paterson shelter starting when she was ten, and now she worked for social services, but he was born later, and they were distracted, and instead of surrounding him in the yolky food of their need to help other people, he was on the outside of the shell, wishing he knew what they really wanted of him.

Never mind that, Timmy thought, because he wasn't one to feel sorry for himself. He looked at Geo, who was flipping through a file folder of photographs as they walked; Timmy had assumed the handlebars of Geo's bike, and thought perhaps they had more in common than the kid could imagine.

"This one," said Geo, holding a photograph of three girls in heavy jackets by the brook. No one was smoking, but their breath puffed out of mouths like speech bubbles.

"Those girls went with her to visit Brown—when she was applying," Timmy said, leaning close to the screen, as if he could touch her.

"Elizabeth and April," he continued. "April is actually going there in the fall." All this mattered so much before, who went where. What Timmy and Linsey had was surety, early decision, an immunity from the posturing and rabid checking of portals at certain hours to see who got into Yale, who got into Emerson, who got into Julliard, who was wait-listed at Swarthmore. It all seemed silly to them then, until she starting thinking about the other schools.

He remembered something she'd told him about that trip. They'd still been together, they were going to be together forever at that point; he was busy pitying people who hadn't found their other half, who didn't get to press their bodies against the bodies that needed theirs. She told him about the guy they stayed with, Cliff—the same guy in that photo from the party. Elizabeth was friends with Celia Savage and Cliff was Celia Savage's stepbrother, and Linsey told Timmy she hadn't known anything, really, about the arrangements, she'd just known that when they arrived, Cliff—who was obscenely handsome, in Timmy's opinion, handsomer than the slightly smarmy Jordan House, but he didn't say that then, he just reminded Linsey that Cliff seemed arrogant—was their host in his off-campus apartment. She'd told him everything, though it was awful, and made him want to hurt this Cliff, and worry about Cliff, and think much more about Cliff than he'd ever wanted to think about another man. His parents had taught him jealousy was like some sort of disease—it damaged people inside, it hurt them and did nothing to give them the objects they desired. Not that Linsey was an object. She said his feeling jealous was cute. He kissed her too hard.

She'd recounted the night they stayed over, after Elizabeth and April had gone to sleep beside each other in the pull-out couch, like a married couple. Linsey left her air mattress on the floor and went back into the kitchen. Cliff was looking over his pharmacology textbook, but she knew he'd been waiting for her. Here she told Timmy she never thought of another boy, that she wasn't even thinking of Cliff, she was just unable to sleep. Linsey said this and they both knew that she was trying to make him jealous, that she wanted him to fight for her, that she wanted to feel safe knowing he would dig his fingers into the flesh of the world to keep her.

"You shouldn't flirt with me," Cliff had said. "Come here," he said, waiting for her to come, then placing her hands on his shoulders. "I'm very stiff."

She knew that was a dirty thing to say, she told Timmy, watching his face, and she wasn't flirting, she really wasn't, but all the same she rubbed his shoulders.

They were very stiff, she told Timmy, ridiculously huge shoulders. *Cro-Magnon shoulders,* she said, laughing.

"I told you not to flirt with me," Cliff said, putting his hands over hers. *I was just being friendly.* Timmy had felt his jaw ache. He'd told her to stop telling the story, but she wouldn't.

"Why shouldn't I flirt?" she said she'd asked him, though she was asking Timmy just now, wanting him to tell her because of me, wanting him to say because it makes me rageful, jealous, furious, aroused.

"You don't know me, that's why," Cliff had said. He peeled her hands off his shoulders, as if it had been her idea all along.

He laughed a little, standing and steering her toward the room where her friends slept.

"Besides, you're jailbait."

"And that was that," Linsey had said to Timmy.

"I wish you wouldn't," said Timmy, unable to look at her

face. She had been wearing a button-down blouse. Bright blue. He fiddled with her top button.

"What, flirt? You know I'd never cheat on you."

"I wish you wouldn't tell me stories like that."

There he was in Geo's photograph, the boy, the Cro-Magnon. He asked Geo to e-mail it to him as they parted ways on the corner of Cedar Court and Sycamore. It was time to visit Linsey's mother.

24 SYCAMORE STREET

The young man had started coming over every day with his cello, leading it up the street as if he was walking a dog. It reminded Mr. Leonard of the conservatory; it reminded him of his childhood, when there were always the bodies of instruments warming the rooms along with their players. When he knew all their voices more clearly than the English language, the flutes' insistences, the violas' womanly complaints. Jordan House was a talent of some sort—Mr. Leonard couldn't read how great—but he was lost in language, lost in the forest of his own expectations. Mr. Leonard knew it, he knew what depression looked like from inside: You go to the store and no one knows, no one knows what you're going through. Your mother is dead. Your lover married someone else. You have cancer. They just know they're looking for the Downy laundry detergent and you're in their way at the Wisk.

Jordan brought the cello and played whatever parts he could for Mr. Leonard, transcribing as he played, a beautiful skill; Mr. Leonard had never fully mastered it. They hardly talked, mostly they just played. It had been after the police took him in—the young man had come to his door with his instrument, stood and spoke through the screen, "Mr. Leonard? I'm Jordan House. I'm a lapsed musician, and I just want someone to play with." Like the men who used to come with knife-sharpening vans, to your door, asking to sharpen your knives. Only this was a better kind of commerce.

Mr. Leonard wrote at night. His hands felt brittle now, as if they'd been frozen and thawed one time too many. Some days they shook as he marked the notes on the pages, dashing the connection of their stems, up, down, connected triplets, trying to keep it all before it was gone. But this time, it wasn't disintegrating after he woke—it stayed with him, clear in his head, all the voices, clearer than the water sounds from outside, the trees underwater, the wind saturated, the air itself swallowed up in ocean.

The cancer made him feel both substantial and fragile, like a snowflake, like the finest of laces, eaten out but holding, a skeleton, a dried sponge. Mr. Leonard was writing again, he was composing, and it was working this time, the music was coming through his dreams, through his fingers onto the page, a complete conduit, a full circuit.

He had relinquished the formality of food, but he had lollipops and afternoon jasmine tea. In the mornings he spoke to the piano, and then started a lollipop, grape or orange, the satisfying snap as the plastic wrapper came off in a single piece. He let the sticks collect in cups, like flower stems. His mother died without this declination, the long letting go.

If Mr. Leonard's mother had lived long enough, say five or six months longer, then Mr. Leonard would have a sister. A souvenir of his mother, he thought, but he tried to think it aslant, not looking his own selfish thought in the eye. She would've lived with him now, he knew this with certainty. Maybe she'd be divorced or widowed, but she'd be home again with him by now in his convalescence and simultaneous blooming. It was unkind to think of his mother this way, he was sure, to blame her, but he held the second loss like a cup full of water. Drink, let it go. He needed his hands above all else, for playing, for writing, for holding the music fast to the pages before he was emptied from the world. He didn't mind death. Sometimes he minded knowing so many other deaths—his mother, his father, his aunt, his sister who never made it out of the womb.

He found out at his father's funeral, over a decade ago. His aunt had come back from Vienna, where she'd lived for six years with a woman who may or may not have been her lover. She smelled of the lavender water she would use sparingly until her own death, because it was the last bottle from the last trip to the last store. His aunt liked finality. At his father's funeral she had a strange grin, almost a smirk. She'd finished her modest speech about her brilliant older brother from the podium at Carnegie Hall, where they were holding a memorial service. They had cast the ashes off the Palisades into the Hudson, his aunt pitching her handful like wedding rice. She spoke about the comfort of his shadow, and she'd come to sit beside Mr. Leonard, grasping his hand as if he were a mooring or a sea-tossed ship, he wasn't sure which. Her hands were chapped but warm. She didn't let go until the reception. The stylish desserts were too festive for a funeral, but they were eating them with abandon, the first violins, the composers, the opera directors, the fraternal students with their same wide jaws and lost gray eyes. They ate the obscenely glazed fruit tarts and the tiny opera cakes, their chocolate layers and strawberry delineated like geologic finds.

"You know," his aunt said, her hand sliding from his and into her lap, "he always called me a minor talent."

"A minor talent?" It was so mean, Mr. Leonard's breath hurt. His aunt had played for years in Europe, never building much of a career, but occasionally appearing with her famous brother's orchestras, occasionally concertizing for a university benefit. She taught, and was renowned for shepherding prodigies onto the stage without letting them lose themselves in fame. His father had said something about that. He had said she was an expert in holding them back just enough to never make it. Mr. Leonard didn't share this with his aunt.

"A minor talent is better than C major talent," he said.

His aunt grimaced, then her face broke free of its distress and she smiled.

"I wish you had had that sister," she said. She cuffed her hand over her mouth. He knew she was pretending; he knew she'd wanted to tell, and tell she did. His mother had been hoping to announce her pregnancy to his father, to young Mr. Leonard himself, at her birthday celebration at the end of the summer. Blueberry pies, they always had blueberry pies. Champagne for the parents and sparkling cider for Mr. Leon-

ard. That year, of course, there was no pie. But she would've
told him there was someone coming into the world to keep
him company after his parents were gone.

"Part of the autopsy," said his aunt. *"Auf gut Deutsch.*
That's how he found out." She had a bit of Vienna in her
now—she said "the plain truth" as "the good German."
"May've been the pregnancy that killed her, that made her
immune system so sensitive." His aunt was tipsy with grief
and the pleasure of relinquishing her secrets. He knew this
was pure conjecture.

"C sharp major talent," said Mr. Leonard, his chest hurting more from the sister he'd just lost than from his father,
who had been gone awhile before it was official.

She would come to live with him, his aunt; they would
husband the old house like a couple, like brother and sister.
Only she told him what to do more than a sister would, he
thought—she bothered him with formalities, with washing
his hands before dinner, with whether he'd returned his
library books on time. Still, they had been perhaps the easiest
years of his life, his aunt's clattering in her own room, typing
letters on an Underwood, irritating the neighbors by going
out for the newspaper in her stockings with garters showing
when the wind gapped her robe. Stockings and a robe, bare
feet and a careful felt hat, that was his aunt to the last. He'd
not expected her to die, despite all evidence that no one in his
life was permanent. Now he understood it, though, the relief
of finishing one's work, the relief of not having to fight all the
gravities of daily life. Of knowing your own difference and

forgetting it in the slick work of walking on the sidewalk in unfrozen February.

One afternoon they were playing with the windows open. Usually, he kept them closed now; usually he wanted to keep the inside air contained—it felt safer that way. He knew his house smelled stale. Other than writing and playing his music with Jordan, there wasn't much left for him. He couldn't eat without the welling up of a terrible nausea. He had put the gowns in a trunk and labeled them "Mother's Things" as if he'd never opened them, as if he'd never folded himself inside the fabric. He couldn't now, anyway, he couldn't move from room to room without working in small starts, or without Jordan's help when he was there. Sometimes, he waited on the floor, touching the hallway's tongue and groove, keeping his pad with him, two pencils in case one point dulled too quickly. He never locked his door—if someone came to hurt him, it would be easy work just to let them.

"You need a nurse," said the young man, having just carried him to the bench, propped him up with pillows.

"I am dying, Jordan," he said. "And it's rather nice this way. Playing to the end."

"Just don't do it while I'm here, okay? I wouldn't want anyone to blame me."

"Hah," said Mr. Leonard. "Back to the second movement. Much more agitato. I know it's hard to play violin on the cello—"

"It isn't. It's fine. You need more juicy cello sections, though."

What Mr. Leonard wasn't telling him was that he had a cello concerto upstairs, his other final work, in the drawer of the bedside table. It wasn't just for Jordan; his mother had loved the cello—it sounded like her voice. But he wasn't planning to hear this piece except in his own head until after he was dead. He was rather looking forward to it.

Since he hardly ate, he didn't have to go to the bathroom, not often. He drank sparingly, enough to keep from becoming powder before he'd finished these last two pieces—the cello concerto for his mother, and the symphony, which was for his father and his unborn sister. The swollen voice of strings, the timpani interrupting, the woodwinds and the sweetest flute song that was for her. It wasn't painful anymore. He had music; he had something to finish, and something to look forward to at last.

Jordan was pecking out the flute part now, on the piano because Mr. Leonard was in the chair, scribbling down some more for the finale. It was coming before the end of the second movement, but he was upright, he needed to transcribe.

"It sounds like a girl, a lost girl," said Jordan.

Mr. Leonard bit the inside of his cheek. The blood tasted sweet, just a little blood.

"They still haven't found her," Jordan said, looking out the window at Linsey Hart's house. "I'm sorry," he added. "I know they gave you a hard time—I wasn't implying anything—"

"It's all right," said Mr. Leonard. His fingers were dented

from the pencil; he massaged them, trying to get back enough circulation to write more. "I know something I didn't tell them," he said.

Jordan played the flute again, more fluently. He looked at the page and the keys, only. He was an awkward pianist, unaccustomed to the horizontal surface of sound.

"It was old news, so I thought it didn't matter. Doesn't matter." He sucked in air against his teeth, annoyed by the restraints of tense.

"Okay," said Jordan. He plucked out the violin line, the melody, much too slowly.

"One night, maybe last year, she sat under my window with that boyfriend of hers, Timmy."

"The one she broke up with?"

"She didn't break up him."

Jordan stopped playing and looked at the man, quizzical.

"That part doesn't matter, they said she's not with him. Anyway, they sat under my window. I was looking over Rachmaninoff—not playing, just thinking it, because sometimes they mind if I play at night."

"And?"

"And do they think houses are anonymous at night? Teenagers. I was right there, and they were talking under my window. She said she'd pretend to break up for her mother— so she'd leave them alone."

"Ah." Jordan was studying his strings. "What did the boyfriend say?"

"He dissembled for a while, but eventually he said maybe

the mother was right—they shouldn't stretch things across the continent."

"Poor kid," said Jordan. He looked out the window as if there were more information there.

"And she sobbed. That girl, she had been left too many times, I think. She said maybe she'd go to school in California, or maybe she wouldn't go to school at all. I hope no one took her—I hope she finds a way to do what she needs to do."

"I hate that idea, that someone *took* her. She's a person—it's so infuriating," said Jordan. "I know that sounds trite. I just hate feeling ineffectual, I hate that someone can have free will taken from them. Even if her free will was going to be something other than what everyone else wanted for her." He spoke as if he knew something about this.

"When you get old, you feel everything becoming ineffectual. I suppose that's the reason for music—someone else's voice singing after you're gone."

"Ah," said Jordan. Mr. Leonard knew he was being kind, a small kindness not to point out how utterly banal his sentiment had been.

"Oh, and she asked her father for money, the night before she left. I heard her call him. I almost called out the window to offer her my money, but that would have been ridiculous."

"So the boyfriend really broke up with her? Did you tell the mother? It might mean something, who knows?"

"I suppose," said Mr. Leonard.

"I could tell them about it—anonymously," said Jordan.

"If you think it matters."

"Everything matters," Jordan said, but he doubted it was true. He looked out the window. There was a cluster of girls in front of the house next door, a young man lying on his back as if their lawn were a beach.

"I think it's supposed to be a vigil," he said. "They don't know how to show support, or else they like the drama."

"Play the adagio again. Strings, please; your piano is awful."

"Is this symphony about her?" He didn't say anything about telling the police.

"Not at all, my dear," said Mr. Leonard. "I'm the only one who's dying now."

3 CEDAR COURT

Geo was constructing a mosaic in the basement, where everything smelled of laundry lint and the clay of underground. He thought she'd be more worried about him, maybe take him to the pediatrician, maybe insist they call the Steins—or at least she'd give him ice and sympathy, but his mother had turned strange on him after she saw the bruise. She'd poked at it for a while, making his skin sting, and then she told him to go clean up his room. He'd hoped they could change the subject, but instead she seemed stuck on his room, and asked him again, and again, when he went to get peanut butter crackers, when he sat upstairs and looked through photographs. He didn't want to; he never wanted to. The mess was organized, and he took comfort in knowing where everything was, even if he didn't know where everything went.

This was why he kept thinking about Linsey, he realized as he carefully sorted bits of sea glass on the basement floor. It was the tangle of simply not knowing. He had collected the sea glass on a trip to Cape May, piles of brown, greens, and cloudy whites, the occasional blue. He was arranging the colors to write Caroline's name, because her birthday would be at the end of the month, and she would come home, and they would mix simple syrup and lemon juice with water, home-made lemonade, the way they did on every one of her birth-days that he could remember.

He was gluing the glass onto a foot measurer from a shoe store, silver and black, numbers and a slide. It was a Bran-nock Device—his father told him, but also the name was etched right in the middle of the numbers and lines. Geo hat-ing having his feet measured. It tickled, and he always imag-ined he was scrunching his feet, giving an incorrect reading. He'd found the tool cast out when the Mom and Pop store two doors down from his father's pharmacy closed. There were piles of shoe boxes, wooden shoe trees, a big bin of rub-ber bands on the curb, and this. He was putting her name on one side of the slide, which was glued into place at the num-ber 20, her age. It would be wonderful and it would make her laugh—and that was what he wanted most.

Some of the edges of the glass weren't quite soft enough; he didn't cut himself, but he pressed his finger against them for the feeling—almost breaking the skin. He squeezed the last of his bottle of craft glue onto the black and stuck in a white moon-shaped piece. Then he went upstairs to see if he could find more glue without alerting his mother to his absence of work on his room cleaning.

"You know"—he could hear her voice on the phone—"it isn't like him."

When he was younger, he always assumed *him* was himself. Now he worried it might be his father. What his father might say about the bruise—why else would Mom be so strange? Geo trod up the stairs, toe to heel, being careful to step once only on each step.

"He won't," she said. She sighed. He had been hoping she would make lasagna for dinner, but she probably wouldn't, now that it was hot out. Oven plus air-conditioning equals waste. Sometimes Geo wouldn't mind a little waste. Why was she harping on his room instead of worrying about his bruise? Had Linsey Hart changed everything?

Mom kept glue in a cabinet in the hallway, along with medicines, and towels, and paper clips, barrettes, and buttons. She was allowed to know where everything was even if there was no conventional order. Why couldn't he do the same with the just-washed bottle caps drying on his rug?

There was no glue in the cabinet, so Geo looked in his parents' room. His mother had a crafting table in the corner, but she usually only used it to pile up books and magazines. She was worse than he was, really, her disorder. He wished he could point this out to her, but instead he walked into her room, squinting with grief at the squeak of the floorboards as he reached the table.

"Aha," he said to himself, collecting a little jar of rubber cement. Underneath it he saw the note he'd run through the wash. She'd said she was giving it to the police, so why was it still here, on her table? He would take it down and remind her. No he wouldn't; she'd tell him to clean his room.

"Bye," he heard her sing into the phone.

Geo stuffed the note into his pocket, but he wasn't fast enough—Mom was on the stairs.

"Geo," she said. "If you clean your room, you can choose what we have for dinner." How did she know his mind?

"Bribery?" he said, trying to distract her from the fact that he was leaving her room, not his own.

"Bribery," she said.

"Fine. Lasagna." Geo went into his own room and closed the door. He opened the crumbling note.

Underneath the bed he found his magnifying glass, the big one with a handle that came with the two-book condensed *Oxford English Dictionary* his father loved. You needed the magnifying glass to read the tiny type, but Geo also needed the magnifying glass for other sorts of work. Like reading the note.

At first he could only make out the words he'd seen before: *Mom* (this could be to anyone), and *new,* and the letter *L.* Maybe *ins.* Maybe he just thought it was *ins* because he wanted it to be Linsey's note. But then, it could be. Everything could be evidence and everything could be nothing. Still peering, fingering the paper, the fibers that had warped with the water and heat of wash and dry, he saw there was a ghost of writing on the folded page, a word that had been written but not inked. There was a *C* and an *A.* There was an *F.* Café? No, there were more letters. He thought of Timmy telling him to make a list of suspects. It was here, in his notebook. Timmy would be gone soon, too—he'd make him something, he thought abruptly. It wasn't that he wanted to be constantly remembered, or even thanked, in particular. He wanted to show that he'd paid attention. It was kind of a reverse mark, like these letters.

Timmy told him Linsey had applied to other schools, schools that would keep her close to Timmy. Why didn't Timmy keep loving her? There were no flaws Geo could see, nothing not to love. He remembered when Timmy told him Linsey should be on her own list of suspects, as if Linsey was capable of crime. *Linsey,* he'd said, *just Linsey.* What if she did something wrong? What if she stole something? What if she'd hurt someone herself? Timmy was moving away, maybe that was the only crack between them. He held the note up to the ceiling light and peered more closely at the soft white paper. And there was the word ghosted on the washed note— he could read it now.

DAY FOUR

36 SYCAMORE STREET

School was starting early this year, before Labor Day. It was the last day of summer, and it felt like a cheat, even to Reeva, who looked forward to the orderly chaos of classes and practices. Summer was a different pace; in summer she was less of a mechanical nagging shuttle bus.

The kids were all out with their friends, wrapped in the arms of fleeting freedoms. The girl was still missing and Reeva felt as though her safety was always uncertain now, the door left unlocked was inviting some sort of loss—of Tina, of Johnny, of secrets. She hated thinking of it, but if Linsey was kidnapped, she'd almost certainly been raped, maybe murdered—it was disgusting. Men were disgusting, the whole idea that someone's child could be touched—it hurt her skin. She found herself checking on Tina several times a day; she looked in on Johnny and wondered how she ever thought she could protect him from the world. What would happen when he got to high school and was still weird? What would happen when he was supposed to get himself up in the morning, when he had to make his own sandwiches? Would he lie on the couch growing thin and old? Would they all come back after college and any freedom she'd found would be crowded back in with people who needed her but didn't necessarily want her around?

The sun wasn't strong enough to etch its way through the smear of clouds, but it was hot out, and chattery with the incessant calls of crickets and cicadas after mates. Dressed for a walk, Reeva was making first-day lunches for tomorrow: Steve liked ham and cheese on the challah rolls from the bakery in Fair Lawn she went to only for challah rolls, Johnny had peanut butter and strawberry jam on white bread—oh, how she hated the sweet chemical smell of white bread—with the crusts cut off. He only ate peanut butter, even though Reeva knew she shouldn't send it in because of all the allergic kids, but there was no other choice. She peeled and sliced his banana, sealing the little container that had held a thousand bananas for her children over the years. She tried to make the slices even. A little box of Yoo-hoo, a concession, because he was supposed to have milk or juice, no sugar except after his homework was done. She was making little concessions now, from waking until sleep she was trying to build a case for forgiveness, trying to insinuate her goodness into the slumbering minds of her family, in case she needed them to let her in again.

Reeva made lunch for Tina, who would probably wad the BLT wrapped in aluminum foil into a fat ball of waste and lob it into the trash. This year, Tina and her friends would have free lunch period once a week; they were allowed, as high school freshmen, to go off campus and into town. Open

Campus, it was called. Last year Steve had used his free lunches to shoot baskets or ride the ramps at his friend Andy's house; Andy's father had built a skateboard haven in his backyard, half guilty, Reeva was sure, because he'd divorced Andy's mother but managed to keep the house and now she lived in a one-bedroom apartment in Waldwick so close to the bowling alley you could hear the hum of the pin-setting machines even with the windows closed (Reeva knew because she'd tried to sell Andy's mother a studio condo in Ridgewood. It was overpriced, but would've kept her closer to home). The other half of the guilt was because Andy had been addicted to heroin for three months during the divorce proceedings, and it took his arrest for the father, an architect who designed the great gray landscapes of Toys "R" Us and Kmart malls, to notice. Andy had a sister with cerebral palsy who lived in a hospital care facility. Andy's father made a game room in the basement, pinball machines and cappuc-cino dispensers, a home theater with angled seating; he'd torn out the mother's former rose and dahlia garden and put in the skateboard ramp.

Steve told his mother he went to Andy's or the Daily Grind, the one remaining nonchain coffee shop in town, during Open Campus, but once last year she'd seen him sit-ting on the corner of Pine and North Dyke Street with the kids who sold pot and test answers, smoking cigarettes. North Dyke, where a client once saw a spectacular old Victo-rian with a new kitchen and new windows and a finished basement playroom and a mother-in-law suite that was sell-

ing for below market value because there'd been an accident
in the backyard with one of the contractors and a circular
saw and everyone knew and the homeowners were supersti-
tious, and the clients had asked, staring at the listing sheet,
"Has anyone ever petitioned the city council for a name
change for the street? I mean, North *Dyke*, it's horrible—that
would certainly be a factor—"

People were so pathetic. There was Steve on North Dyke.
She'd stopped her car. She'd been the mortifying mother
who dragged her son away from trouble by the ear, literally,
his flaccid ear that drooped as it always had, since infancy.
Steve told her he'd been smoking for six months, just cigarettes, but he wanted to quit anyway for track. She watched
him until he did.

This year it was Tina's turn, and the sad news for Reeva
was that Tina would go where all her girlfriends went, and
that where was Starbucks. She hated the thought of Jordan
eyeing her daughter, of her daughter checking out her ex-
lover, of the cross purpose of secrets. She tucked a Toblerone
bar from her own secret stash into Tina's lunch bag. Concessions.

This morning Reeva had waited for Charlie to get out of
bed, to crack his knuckles and his neck, to gargle and preen
and go, but he hadn't. She mumbled, she rolled around in the
bed; she tugged at his cocoon of striped cotton sheet.

She loved Charlie. She loved how he brushed his teeth,
scrubbing with the battery-operated brush like a five-year-
old demonstrating his prowess for the dentist. It wore at his

gums, that concentrated attention. And he'd given her that same attention; when they were dating, he wouldn't leave her alone. When they'd been in college, in statistics class together, she'd known he was watching for her when she entered the stadium classroom designed for the one hundred-plus students fulfilling their requirement while chewing Dentyne gum and checking their day planners for the rest of the day's pursuits. He could see her from the front row, without turning, but he turned, he always turned toward her like a plant drawn to light, like an infant's fingers wrapping to touch. He'd come to her dorm room, one of the few all-women's dorms on campus, and he'd stood by the buzzer waiting to be let in, every single day after they started dating, every day until his appendix burst, and he called her from the hospital before surgery, because he'd listed her as next of kin on his intake forms and wanted her to know.

Maybe that's what she missed, maybe she missed Charlie more than she missed Jordan, maybe it was just that she hadn't been in someone's absolute vision, someone's necessity, for so long. Last had been her baby Johnny, and now even he didn't need her, even though his needs extended past the ordinary scope of arms.

Charlie didn't move. Charlie, who was always up early, even when they went on vacation. Charlie, who slept through every night feeding of every child but rolled over and began popping his joints at five forty-six without fail. Now, he was failing. At first, she was irritated. She had wanted him to leave so she could fall into the deeper sleep she had when she had the bed to herself. And then she wanted him to leave so she could think about Jordan in the half-lit mind of early morning that allowed her to touch herself without guilt. It was just the work of the body, it wasn't any real intention.

Jordan, Jordan, she thought. Charlie would be crushed about Jordan, he must never find out about Jordan. She loved Charlie too much to have done what she did with Jordan. And then she felt it, desire. Because even though she'd banished him from the workings of her waking day, Jordan was very real in her imaginary sex life, and it wasn't her fault entirely, it was her limbic system. Maybe she had an appendixlike evolutionary impetus.

"Charlie," she finally said, whispering as if someone else was sleeping with them. "You're going to be late."

"What?" Charlie stopped breathing. He'd been nose whistling. Not quite snoring.

"You're going to be late," she said. Then added, "Honey." She patted the striped sheet near his arm.

"Not going," said Charlie. "I told you, I took a few days off this week. Slow." He grunted and rolled over to her, his arm across her shoulder. Close to her breast, not touching. His breath was strangely sweet, like Johnny's grape toothpaste. For a minute, she let herself imagine her husband kissing her son's mouth, the transfer of glittery grape. Ick. Not her fault, her restless mind. She wasn't enjoying her body's betrayal; she was warm, she was horny, she was used to sex now, to lots of sex, and she was thinking about Jordan's legs as Charlie swung his atop hers.

"But I think I'll go for a run," he said.

"You've been running a lot," she said, just noticing now. When had it changed from once or twice a month on the weekend? This summer? Charlie hadn't exercised at home in years, preferring the gym at work, where she imagined him tugging away at the pulleys and levers of ancient exercise equipment, a towel around his neck, the clock on the wall erasing the potential of that singular billable hour. He brought home his gym bag once a month, and the sweatshirt and sweatpants hardly bore evidence of great effort. But still, he was in decent shape, for his age. He ran once a month or so, weekend warrior, and she always thought of it as an excuse to not ferry the kids to their practices and games; to not accompany her to Stop & Shop, which he did sometimes, lagging behind her cart like an eight-year-old, tossing fried onion rings into the basket to piss her off. Maybe to tease her.

Then he was standing, stretching his sinewy legs, bending with the stiff effort of a man who had just been sleeping. He was wearing only boxer shorts, and she was watching him, the extra fat that had settled around his belly, the hairy mole on his back where it bent. He was bouncing, making curt, old movements. His eyes were slightly crusty and the hairs on his thighs were at least half gray. He was bouncing, and she imagined his muscles tearing a little with each brittle tug. His shorts were red tartan and worn, and the fly gapped open as he put his hands on his hips, tugged his waist forward and back, a stiff old gym teacher. She could see his penis moving against the fabric, the remnants of a morning erection making the little mouth of the opening talk to her.

Finally, he was gone. She wasn't horny anymore. Or if she was, she didn't deserve to be. She was out of bed and seeing the kids off to their pursuits. She was drinking coffee and sorting out the fridge, almost as though her husband had gone off for an honest day.

And there she was in the kitchen when Charlie came home with his shirt damp, his legs looking younger for their work. He leaned on the counter and looked at her; she could feel herself blush under the scrutiny.

"Would you like coffee?" she asked. She wasn't sure how she would make it through this day with him, what they would have to say to each other. She'd had plans. Ordinary plans, perhaps, but plans nonetheless. She'd planned to go to the bank, to stop by Lord & Taylor for bonus days on her favorite cosmetics. She'd planned to walk down Sycamore, almost past 6½, but not quite that far, because although she hoped Jordan might see her, she didn't want to see him—this same theory held for parking at the bottom of town and walking up to the bank, past Starbucks; she wanted to be seen through the tinted glass, but not to engage—and besides, she was going to stop by the Steins' house. She wanted to see how Abigail was holding up. She had dressed in her pink and green dress from the Lilly Pulitzer store she'd bought with a gift certificate Charlie gave her—a Chamber of Commerce certificate, so unspecific he hadn't even chosen a store, for god's sake. Still, the dress looked good on her, in a WASPy,

I've got something you want but I probably won't give it up willingly sort of way. She liked that, with lipstick ordinarily too dark for the end of August. And while it was sexy in a way only certain men understood, it wasn't inappropriate to wear to call on a neighbor in crisis. Which Abigail was. There was something about the way she'd leaned against Reeva's door frame, when Reeva had told her about Mr. Leonard, that made her want to talk more, to unravel, to be someone to lean on. She didn't care about the gossip or the details in particular; she honestly wanted to help someone. It might make her a better person.

She sighed as she stuffed old spaghetti into the disposal. Charlie flipped through the newspaper, but she could tell he wasn't reading.

"Want to go out?" he asked. Reeva felt a prickle at the backs of her knees and reached down to scratch. But it wasn't an itch, it was something familiar, a specific sort of surprise, almost arousal, she used to feel around Charlie. Her skin tense with the possibility of touch.

"Out? Oh, I had somewhere to go—" She left him at the counter, bending his knees back, stork.

"I thought we could go to Starbucks," her husband said. "We could sit and drink coffee and talk, like grown-ups sometimes do—" He was watching her, but she couldn't turn to meet his eyes.

"Hmm," she said, striding up the stairs. She should say yes, she should. Small concessions. She stopped at the landing, turned. Charlie was in the living room now, doing back-overs, pressing his yellowish toenails into her carpet. There was something about all that exertion that made her proud of him, and she reached, trying to remember what it was like to feel proud of him as a man, not a partner, not a father, not just the moneymaking part of the team. His back was long and powerful; he didn't really look old. He wasn't old. She wondered how other women saw him.

Then she went into the bathroom, to check her makeup, to reach back and unbuckle her bra. She didn't need a bra in this dress, and suddenly she felt restricted. She pulled it out through the armholes by the strap and went to the bedroom, noticing a smudge on the window. She wiped at it with a tissue. Maybe he'd just go off for coffee by himself. Let him go to Starbucks and see their daughter there, nursing a crush on the man his wife had been sleeping with. Her stomach was tight. She was so foolish. It wasn't guilt she was feeling, though she should have felt guilt, it was heat. The limbic system, she remembered, sex, food, fight. Hers was overactive, she was sure. She rubbed at the smudge on the window, but it wouldn't come off.

"Hey," said Charlie. She hadn't noticed he'd followed her into the bedroom. "I like that dress."

His erection was obscene through the jogging shorts, smooth yellow nylon from 1980-something when he'd last been a regular jogger. It was admirable, actually, he was admirable. She wanted to know what he saw in her, whether he could sense the lines of the dark red *A* under her skin. And she did love him, though she didn't understand why he was home, for the first time without making some elaborate vacation plan, or some golf outing, in at least ten years.

"Hey," he said again. Now he was pressing against her, feeling her breasts. She wanted to stop him; she wanted to tell him she'd cheated on him, but it was over. Her body, however, didn't want anything of the kind. She had never lost her morning arousal, and as he reached around to rub her, she cried out, coming almost before his fingers started to work. The window wasn't covered. She looked out at the street, at a bag of grass clippings from the Hopsmiths' yard spilling out onto the sidewalk, at a fat robin hopping on one leg as if injured. She came again as he touched her and she wasn't able to be quiet, she was yelling, but it felt as though someone else was making the noise, someone else was enjoying this. Charlie was, at least, he had pulled her dress up from behind, had entered her, was groping her with intensified intention.

"You like that?" he said. "You're a little wild today."

She couldn't say anything, she might give something away. Could he tell her body was different? She thought she could smell Jordan, only it was her husband's fingers in her mouth. And now he was pulling her hair, working against her and into her, and telling her she was bad, a bad girl, the way he often did, because he thought she liked it, only this time he was telling the truth.

They lay down on his favorite striped sheets. She was still dressed. She tugged her underpants back on and was thinking about whether or not she still had time to pick up the dry cleaning today. It kept her from saying anything. If she said anything, it might be the wrong thing. If she said anything, she might make a mistake.

"Well," said Charlie. "You certainly made my day off." He kissed her hands. She looked at the ceiling. They'd had it painted just two years ago, but already there was a web-thin crack around the light fixture.

"Are you okay?" He rolled over, looked at her face. She glanced at him, but it felt too dangerous to answer, so she just nodded.

"Good," he said. "Jogging is clearly good for me." He was flexing his legs now, enjoying his own muscles. Reeva laughed. It was a relief.

"I guess maybe we could go out to lunch instead of that coffee?" she said. When had they gone out to lunch last—a thousand years ago? She used to come in to Hackensack, to meet him at the mall for lunch. They'd discussed orthodontia and new bikes at the food court. Once they'd even gone to a matinee, but after he became partner, he couldn't leave for that long and she'd stopped. She remembered the sweet sesame oil taste of the noodles he liked. She licked his fingers, which tasted of her.

He had been more aggressive than usual, he had been so purposeful. She wondered whether he'd planned the days off as sex days, the way they used to plan their sex for the tiny slot of time on Sundays when all the kids had playdates or pickup games. He called it Sunday school. She told him she needed to catch up on her catechism. Why had she forgotten all this? Why had she ever cheated on him, crumpled up their past like newspaper around dog shit? She started chewing on her fingernail, a habit she'd broken in grade school with Lee Press On Nails and desire.

"You know who I saw when I was jogging? Abigail Stein. She's holding up pretty well, though they still don't know where her daughter went."

Reeva bit her cuticle, and it started to bleed. "I hope it wasn't an abduction," she said. Abduction sounded like abortion. Maybe she'd been pregnant. That Abigail Stein was so hard to read, but it couldn't be easy. Reeva remembered when she told Beth about Johnny's ADD how Beth had nodded her head, so sage, so superior, and said, "Someday they'll figure out it was something the mothers did when they were pregnant." As if Reeva weren't Johnny's mother. As if that weren't an accusation.

"They don't know," he said. "I was thinking we might need an alarm system. What do you think?" He was running his hands through his hair now, sitting up, looking in the mirror. Did he have a thing for Abigail Stein? Impossible. She was pretty enough, but far from his type. She hardly wore makeup, and her eyebrows were so thick. When did she start jogging? Reeva tried to imagine her neighbor in motion, those large breasts swaying as she moved. Jealousy nicked at her organs, a small, vicious animal. She looked at her husband, wondering. Had he been thinking about Abigail Stein while he was taking her from behind at the window? No—she was the cheater; she was the one who had thoughts like that.

"She's holding up well," he said again, and Reeva could imagine him then, holding up those big breasts. Her neck was stiff and her thighs were sore and even though she had come, several times, maybe she only enjoyed the idea of it; the actual action didn't work as well for her as she'd hoped. He was her husband, for god's sake, they'd had sex a million times at least ("Be specific," Charlie might say. "Is it actually a million?") and now he was talking about Abigail Stein, who was supposed to be part of *her* day, not part of his day. Sex made her want to weep, made her want to be moved, made her angry and anxious and satisfied all at the same time. Jordan would've left for town already; she was too late to be seen on her way to the Steins' house. She was not going to think about him anymore, and she was not going to help Abigail Stein because clearly Abigail already had friends enough. Reeva pulled a bra from the drawer.

"I liked it without," her husband said, leering at her. No, he was being sexy, he was being sweet.

"Where do you want to go for lunch?" she asked, wrestling the bra back into place.

There was a clatter in the hallway; the heavy hoofbeats of one of her children come inside downstairs. Reeva left the bedroom before she could change her mind again.

"Ma," said Tina, standing at the foot of the stairs, gripping the BLT in foil like a dirty diaper. "What's in here?"

"Your lunch for tomorrow," said Reeva, sighing.

"I already ate the carrots," said Tina. There was chocolate on her chin. That, too, thought Reeva. Still, Tina was so clean, so unlined, so fresh in her terry mini and tank top. Reeva thought her daughter might have sex soon, and the thought made her want to vomit. She gagged a little.

"I can't believe you wrapped it in foil," said Tina. "It's so wasteful. Why didn't you just use cellophane?"

Reeva gasped, maybe because of the nausea, maybe because her daughter had used the word. Since when did Tina say cellophane? She said *plastic wrap*. She didn't say cellophane. Only Jordan said cellophane. Her daughter turned away, eating her sandwich and swishing back into the kitchen. The skirt was too short. Her shirt was too tight; her beauty made it difficult for Reeva to fill her lungs with breath.

26 SYCAMORE STREET

Since the newspaper article, the teenage girls—and occasional sheepish boy—had hovered about the Stein house, leaving only between the hours of midnight and nine or ten, when they sat on the curb drinking coffee—and, upon occasion, smoking, which Abigail found contemptible. Who let their kids smoke—and out in the world? It was a vigil— Mom's green-tea-jasmine-scented forty-dollar candles in hand, little bouquets of flowers from gardens or plastic blossoms from the Rite Aid clustered around an enlarged, laminated copy of the paper with the graduation photo. It reminded Abigail, nauseatingly, of a highway shrine.

In fact, she overheard Tina Sentry this morning, sitting cross-legged on the sidewalk atop what was probably a two-hundred-dollar cashmere throw, talking to a friend who wore brown lipstick and teeny tiny shorts with a crop top, scarlet. "It is totally cool, I am so in favor of this—and you never know who you'll see"—she flicked the pleated end of her skirt as the young man from Starbucks walked past, toward Mr. Leonard's house—"but I like would have preferred, like, a shrine, you know, when you leave the stuff? I mean, it's not like we couldn't still check it out, but a vigil is like, all the time. It would be easier to maintain."

Abigail could feel the *likes* in her throat. She wanted to cut them out of the conversation. This wasn't *like* anything, this was Linsey, missing. All these girls were playing parts. She didn't recognize most of them; Linsey's friends were in college. They were gone, too, only gone in a known way.

She'd always thought of her neighbor Reeva as a queen bee, but she felt the woman's give and take, a little vulnerability, when Reeva told her about Linsey babysitting for her son. The neighborhood was like one of those books Linsey used to love—black-coated sheets with a rainbow beneath; you scraped away at the black with a stylus. Abigail had been irritated by the waxy crumbs, but she'd *oooed* and *aaahed* nonetheless.

Parenthood was waxy crumbs.

Reeva had said she would visit this afternoon. In fact, the past day had been a steady stream of visitors. Abigail wondered if every crisis prompted gifts of food—it felt like shivah, or a wake, and part of her wanted to see no one and part of her appreciated every covered dish, every broccoli-chicken-fettuccine casserole. Beth Boris had just come with seven pies—seven. Who made seven pies? She parked in back—temporarily disrupting the vigil as they parted to let her car through—and brought the pies up in three trips, then one more for a gallon jug of iced tea—*mint!*—because lord knows no one had time to brew during this crisis.

Beth was sweet, but she chattered on like a meandering

stream. She told a story about how her husband had once had her followed, worrying that she was cheating. *It brought them closer!* she said. And she had cystitis. And when her last baby was born she'd had her tubes tied. And she was sometimes a substitute teacher! And she adored the elementary school kids but the middle-schoolers intimidated her! And did Abigail know Reeva Sentry? Reeva had been very weird— they'd been friends, but then Reeva dropped her, and Beth thought perhaps it was because they went to different churches. Was it like that with temple?! Beth put the pies on the counter.

"This is pecan; this is mincemeat, which sounds disgusting but is really good; this is chicken pot pie! Put it in the fridge when it's cool. This is pumpkin! We all need our vitamins. This is creamy, creamy, chocolate peanut butter. You will loooove it. These two are apple. Apple pie. Did I tell you I had a great-great-great-great-something who was on the *Nina*? You know, one of Columbus's boats? I have all this Massachusetts family. Oh, Abby," she breathed, a huge sigh of breath, her body jiggly with breath, her slight second chin pink. "I'm so sorry, I keep talking about me. How are you holding up today?"

"I want to go somewhere. I want to DO something," said Abigail. When Beth called her Abby, it made her whole body itch.

"I know," said Beth. Now she was watching Abigail's face. The stream had stopped suddenly and Abigail felt as though she needed to fill the gap.

"I feel guilty because I still like having sex with my husband," she blurted out. "It's a comfort."

"Oh, honey!" Beth laughed. For a minute, Abigail was mortified. Would Beth take this about the neighborhood, news of Bereaved Abigail Stein and her Secret Sex Life? No, Beth wasn't like that.

"I must leave you. You need some time to yourself. Please don't forget to refrigerate the chicken pot pie. And I'll call on you tomorrow."

"Thank you for everything," said Abigail, standing by the back door. *I wish you would stay. I wish you wouldn't come back.*

She didn't know who to trust, and suddenly everyone was talking to her.

Sometimes she forgot in her dreams, she had told Reeva this yesterday, though she couldn't tell her husband because she felt as though she was betraying everyone—just the act of sleep was enough of a lapse, but then, she dreamed of the summer house her family rented on Lake Michigan one year when she was eleven, the breeze almost like a sea breeze, the white clapboards peeling, the little Sunfish sailboats just offshore made the size of children's toys from the distance. In her dreams, she was with everyone, the boys, Linsey, with her first husband and her second; in her dreams, everyone was intact, and sometimes there was the baby boy she'd lost, too, Joseph Junior, sleeping in a bassinet with a bud mouth working on an invisible nipple. Then she woke out of the sunshine and into the shade-darkened bedroom beside Frank, who was breathing deeply, regularly, and she remembered where she was and that Linsey was gone and she ran to the bathroom to vomit.

It was the first day of school for the boys tomorrow. They were supposed to have taken Linsey to college this weekend; she'd been gone four days and Abigail wept in her daughter's room at night, but she still knew she'd come back, the way she knew her own heart would keep beating despite the weight on her, the thousand thousand pounds of the empty room, of the whole house, of the boys bickering, of her husband trying to find anything, calling, calling, his voice quiet and calm, his heavy arm trying to hold her to the bed at night. She wanted to thank him, wanted to fold herself into him, but mostly, she couldn't forgive him for sleeping, and then she was doing the same, letting them all down by lapsing into it, by falling.

She'd been trying to talk with Joe for two days, after the first call when she told him their girl was missing—a tender call at first, a reasonable bout of terror together. In that one tearful conversation since Linsey went missing, he'd been so supportive, they'd been so connected, and then at the end he questioned her mothering abilities and told her Linsey was probably just out with friends and she should keep better track.

"Out with friends?" she'd said. She knew she was screeching, but she couldn't help it. "Out with friends?"

Joe paused. Joe didn't mind silence if it helped him in an argument. Abigail couldn't bear it.

"Joe?" she asked.

"You wait twenty-four hours to call her father?"

"You're too busy screwing underage soccer players to answer my messages?"

It hadn't been her finest moment, but she couldn't help it. She almost suspected him of being part of this, of knowing something she didn't—his relationship with Linsey had always been slightly opaque to her, and though she did her best to respect it, now she couldn't. She'd asked Barq to check him out, the rotted-apple taste of betrayal rising in her mouth as she made her request. Nothing, so far. Joe was booked for parents' weekend, as she'd suspected, but nothing else.

But that was it. Barq said to keep in touch with him, but the one time Joe picked up his cell phone, he said, "Abigail, unless you have news, I can't talk now." And he'd hung up. What if she'd had news?

She was actually looking forward to talking with Reeva again today. She should be talking to Margaret, or one of her real friends, but somehow Reeva and the neighbors felt safer, more anonymous. Reeva had started telling her something about her periods—it was probably another perimenopause story, and Abigail found those annoying, but the running narrative kept her from falling into her own deep pond. She'd be here soon, and Abigail would probably gush with over-flowing information about how she broke up Linsey and Timmy, how she had dug up the seedlings of their relation-ship. She wanted to confide in someone.. Her house smelled like chicken pot pie with dill. She disliked dill, but the pie would still be delicious. Her mouth was sour; she should keep her business private, there'd already been too much invasion.

Standing by the front window, just out of the line of sight for the vigil clump, Abigail watched a form making his way up Sycamore. She knew that walk: Timmy. Her house was quiet—Frank had taken the boys out for lunch, and had invited her, but the thought of eating made her run into the bathroom for dry heaves. Camp was done. Everyone was home. Linsey should be home.

Her cell phone, turned to maximum, rang and buzzed.

She answered before looking.

"Margaret," she said, interrupting her friend's hello. "God, I'm sorry. I really can't do anything about work now—I have to tell you—"

"Stop," Margaret interrupted in turn. Her voice was sharp. "Honey. Do not keep things from me."

"Oh god," said Abigail. She felt trembly now, weak.

"I don't have a Linsey," she said, "though I desperately wish I did. Don't not let me help."

Abigail was not going to cry. "I am sorry, I am sorry," she said.

"Don't be sorry. Look up the train schedule for me; I'm coming."

Margaret was on her way, which made it all real. It was all real. *I desperately wish I had a Linsey,* Abigail recalled; Margaret had always said she was happy without children.

Abigail had been holding a tea mug all morning—the bergamot of Earl Grey was cold perfume, but she didn't sip.

Timmy was a hero with the gaggle holding a vigil on the lawn. Older from just a few weeks ago, when she'd seen him at graduation, he held his sadness like a man, full fleshed, no more of the boy she'd seen wrapped around her girl, vine around tree. She couldn't see the things that hurt her before, the way he'd been proprietary, the way he'd owned space, and Abigail had worried he was taking Linsey's as well.

Here was a young man, a beautiful young man, loose space at the waist of his jeans, his polo shirt—tie-dyed paradox—accentuating the beauty of his upper body, sinew, strength, sex. Abigail walked to the door but didn't open it. She could hear the girls through the glass, "Timmy! Timmy! Aren't you leaving for California?"

"OMG, Timmy, you must be like, really worried!"

"Timmy? We're sooooo worried for you!" This last was from Tina, Reeva's daughter, who was wearing a string-shouldered tank top and a short skirt. She sat astride one of the boys' old scoot cars, rolling suggestively back, forth. Abigail wanted to go out and cover her up. It wasn't an unkind thing, this vigil, but it was selfish, intrusive. She suspected that when the girls had started gathering last night with their mothers' forty-dollar candles lit, singing tuneless pop songs and holding hands, they wanted to enter the light of the drama, that they didn't actually feel any of the desperation. It wasn't cruel, but it wasn't particularly kind, either.

Abigail swung open the door. She wanted Timmy to know she needed him now. He was supposed to be in California, Abigail knew this from Barq, and from Linsey's excavated texts, and from Timmy's mother, who had called from out of the country somewhere, checking in to see if she could help, the way so many people did, meaning I wish I could help and not I would like to help. But Timmy would like to help.

"Timmy," she called, and her voice cracked. She half-expected the girls to abandon their grassy posts. There was a boy on the lawn with them—he was smoking a cigarette—

"Abigail," said Timmy, very loud, so everyone looked up at this temporary god. "I broke up with her because I broke up with her—it wasn't all you."

He wasn't even all the way up the walkway.

The girls tittered. Abigail wanted to throw something at them, to scream like a mad witch.

"Come in," said Abigail, holding out her hand. "Come in, Timmy," she said, reaching for him.

26 SYCAMORE STREET

The weirdo's going to be in your class this year," said Cody, by means of aggravating Toby, who was scrutinizing his school supplies list at his desk to see if he had everything he needed. Cody had been such an idiot when Dad took them shopping after lunch, sticking candy in the basket when Dad wasn't looking, buying a compass that wasn't on the list because they weren't allowed to use them anymore— because of kids like Cody, Toby thought, who stabbed people with the sharp points. He'd been looking forward to drawing smooth angles; he'd been looking forward to school.

"Who are you talking about?" asked Toby, though he knew he shouldn't take the bait.

"Geography, the Oreo," said Cody, smirking.

"Geo is George, and he's not a weirdo. And it's disgusting to call him names—"

Cody grabbed the list from Toby's hands.

"Why are you being such an asshole?" Toby grabbed the list back, tearing the corner. He could feel the fury building in his chest, fury and grief like a thick hot smoke.

"Ooo, I'm telling Mom you said that," said Cody, wadding up the corner and flicking it at his brother.

"She's not listening," said Toby. "She's talking to Timmy."

There was a brief truceful silence. Timmy had been sitting with Mom in the backyard as if he and Linsey were still together when they'd come home from lunch. They were looking at printouts of e-mail messages and transcripts of texts and Toby felt as though they were conspiring against her, and he ran up to his room. Cody followed, but Cody wasn't in a good mood. Toby could feel his brother's anger in his own skin—like sunburn. He knew Cody had done something wrong; when Cody did something wrong he held it against everyone else until he was found out; his twin was ridiculous that way, so immature. Sometimes everything that was wrong with the world was his brother's fault. He missed Linsey.

Toby tried to breathe. Cody sprawled across his bed, but then he lunged for the desk, scattering Toby's erasers, his newly sharpened pencils, the protractor, the little silver calculator, which hit the floor and cracked.

"To hell with you!" yelled Toby, but Cody dodged out of the room before his brother could lunge at him.

Toby crouched on the floor, picking things up, fury building again. He was going to hit his brother. He was going to pummel him. He'd make him take everything back, the whole last three years or so. He'd make him hurt so much Toby would feel it in his own bones. One pencil was way under his brother's bed, and he moved out the nasty things Cody collected, a box of Yu-Gi-Oh! cards, a dusty pair of socks, the sweater box his mom used to rotate summer and winter things—sweaters had come out a week or so ago, and shorts had gone in—and then he saw it through the plastic, the familiar shape of Linsey's monkey box, hidden among the blue of his brother's shorts.

Toby took it out, opened the lid, looked inside at the little talismans of his sister's life, holding them like religious objects: a baby tooth, a gold heart charm—

"MEME!" screamed Cody, diving atop his brother. It was a word from Speakey, their lost language. They'd used it as babies to mean Mom, or even milk; embarrassingly enough, it meant their mother's breasts. But after that it meant *mine,* it was the first word of their division. *Meme,* Cody said, all the time; he'd wanted everything.

"MEME!" his brother yelled again, boring his hands into Toby's, grabbing for everything. Toby managed to scratch just above his brother's collarbone, and watched the welt rise with disgust and satisfaction.

"Why did you take it? It's not yours, what did you do?" Toby relinquished his grip on the box, but he held the charm, the tooth, gripping them in fists he tried to use. Cody was all knees and elbows, all harm. Something made contact with Toby's hip, and it hurt, but not enough to stop his fury.

"Fuck you," said Cody, suddenly still, staring at Toby's face. Toby's eyes stung. For once, his brother was paying attention. "I loved her, too."

"Never said you didn't," said Toby, the tooth cutting into his palm, his hip throbbing.

"You act as if she belonged to you."

"Quit saying things like that. She's not dead."

"I don't know," said Cody, standing up, taking the box with him. "Those guys usually chop up their victims." He left the room with the box, and though Toby was tempted to follow him, he was too bruised to go on with this.

"She's not dead," he told the gold heart charm in one hand, the tooth in the other. He let his guilty, thieving brother go. *Meme,* he thought. He would have taken the box himself if he'd had the chance.

3 CEDAR COURT

Geo's mother had gone out to meet a friend; his father was at work. Merry thudded around her room, reciting the last of her summer poetry reading list, Louise Gluck, "You have only to wait/they will find you," hollering it as if volume could help her absorb the material into her blood. He'd promised his mother he would tell her when he was going, so she could watch, but he couldn't do it if he knew she was watching, so he'd have to tell her afterward, he'd have to disappoint her just this much. Otherwise he'd never make it.

Geo perched atop his father's still-spring-crusty Wellingtons to spy on his neighbors through the mudroom window. First the boys ran into the house with their father behind them, Mr. Stein carefully locking his car with a key, though surely it had a remote. He could see Mrs. Stein through the window, talking with Timmy, then Timmy and Mrs. Stein sequestered in the backyard as if they'd be safe there—from what, Geo didn't know, perhaps the scrutiny of the vigil or the ears of the twins.

Then Cody left for some practice or other, yelling unintelligible good-byes to his house as he circumnavigated the girls on the lawn and slammed the door of the car pool Volvo. Boys with shin guards and numbered shirts cluttered the backseat. They waved at the girls—one of the girls called out, "We don't know anything! But we're praying!" It worried Geo, this perky discussion.

Then Reeva Sentry walked up to the front door with a bouquet of flowers—lilies, Geo noted, that would smell like rot as soon as they began to droop. When no one answered the door, Reeva turned to the group and said something to her daughter, Tina. Tina was swishing her short skirt as though there were invisible bulls to tempt. Reeva's face soured, but she walked up the driveway to the backyard where Geo knew Abigail and Timmy conferred.

Geo's heart slammed against his chest in anticipation. He wasn't sure if he was relieved or terrified that he'd convinced his mother to let him go alone.

At least his mother hadn't reported the fence-slat incident to the police yesterday as she handed over the note to the detective in the blue, short-sleeved button-down. At least the detective—who'd asked him where it came from, who'd asked him what he knew of Linsey Hart, and who had watched his eyes so intently Geo was afraid to look around the living room, as if he was hiding something in the otto-man, the piano, the wedding photo on the mantel, his bat-tered shoes by the French doors to the office—at least the detective hadn't asked him about the welt above his collar. He had, however, asked him about friends. About Cody, and Toby, about whom he played with and what they said. And he

thought about play, about how glad that in a few years he'd be
old enough to be with people without the expectation of
engaging in their sorts of play, or sports—that he wouldn't
have to like football or soccer or lacrosse. He'd be old enough
so conversation was sufficient, or simply being together, the
way he'd been with Minal. He'd probably loved her.

He had friends, but no one like Minal. No one with
whom he felt no need to talk to fill the empty space between
faces. For much of fourth grade he'd been what one might
have called best friends with Donny Apple, a round-faced
boy almost as tall as their teacher, Miss Bestie. Donny's face
grew plum in gym class, and in third grade Cody and Banks
and the other boys who seemed to feed on teasing the way
catfish fed on bottom scum had razzed Donny. Stole his
lunch sometimes. Stuck Post-it notes on his back that read
KIK ME or FAT ASS. Sometimes they got detention. There
were three all-school assemblies that year about zero toler-
ance and antibullying, but Donny would never squeal, and
mostly, they never got caught.

By fourth grade Donny was so big no one messed with him
anymore. It was as though turning red with exertion or having
a face shaped like a playground ball were no longer offenses.

Geo liked Donny because Donny drew elegant sketches
of robots and spaceships and sometimes, when he thought no
one saw his doodles, of the other kids in class. He gripped his
pencils with Cheetos-stained, bent fingers, pressing into the
yellow edges of the wood as though it might fly off without
mammoth pressure. He got Rebecca Boolie's nose perfect,

not quite upturned, but open at the bottom. He drew a picture of Toby Stein, capturing the *O* expression he always held in his mouth during recess kickball games.

Donny came over to Geo's house, and they played Yahtzee and Clue and Jenga at the table. Geo's mother brought them oatmeal cookies and Donny picked out the raisins, hoarding them in his fist under the table, then handing them to Geo like a secret. Geo told him his mother wouldn't care, but Donny was afraid of causing offense.

Donny's house was in the fanciest part of town, where the Victorians sat on one-acre lots like spiders fat in their webs. His mother was an executive trainer and left the house before daylight most mornings. His father was some kind of traveling salesman—Geo never knew what he sold, but he was only home twice a month for two days. The nanny was from Poland, a young woman with short blond hair and tired eyes, and halfway through the year's friendship she was replaced by her sister, who had boyfriends over to the house and whose eyes were so green she looked as though she'd come from another planet, not another country. Most of the house was immaculate, bronze statues in the living room that looked out from tiny holes in their eyes—Donny told Geo they were like giant pupils, those holes—and curtains the maid vacuumed every day. Seven people lived in the house: Donny; his brother, Ralph, who was twenty; his mother; the nanny; the maid; the cook, and his wife, whom they all called Auntie, and who never came out in daylight. She knit in the basement apartment, coming up once in a while with a new sweater made from alpaca wool or silk yarn, cowl-necks, cabled cardigans, all absurdly colorful for school.

The best part of Donny's house was the swimming pool in the back, inside what used to be a greenhouse, and which still smelled green. The second best part of Donny's house was the dining room table, which the maid and nanny referred to as "the pile," and which they were not allowed to organize. The table was piled at least four feet high with objects and papers. Once, Donny had asked his mother for a copy of his birth certificate, to prove to Geo that he had been born in Manhattan, though Geo had asked for no such proof, and his mother, who was home at seven PM for once because it was Parents' Night at the school, reached deep into the pile with her eyes closed, like a diviner led by a rod, and pulled out Donny's birth certificate. "Donald Purpose Exeter Apple II" it read. He had been born in Manhattan, but that impressed Geo far less than the pile. Gas bills, a pleated red silk lampshade, a plum pit, a fish skeleton mounted on a slab of mahogany, an avocado tree sprouting from a pit in a cracked clay pot, several of Auntie's sweaters, Donny's first-grade plaster cast of his face, Ralph's report cards, a blood test report from when Donny's mother was pregnant with Donny, a Havahart mousetrap smeared with peanut butter, every drawing the boys ever brought home from school, sepia photo portraits of Donny's grandparents, passports, dollar bills, euros, yen, credit card bills, pot holders, a pulled wisdom tooth, what looked like a urine sample, pill bottles, a rubber doorstop, chocolate coins, several copper pots.

Donny wasn't going to be in his class this year. They'd see each other on the playground, but Geo knew he'd have to invite himself over if he wanted to see the pile again, if he wanted to play chess in the basement.

Geo had never noticed the flagstones on the Steins' walkway, the way they were a smooth mosaic, a serpentine shape of irregular triangles, hexagons, lopsided ovals, and cement. He recognized a girl from the middle school who wrote articles for the student paper. She waved with her hand low, as if to only salute his feet.

"Hi," whispered Geo. He didn't have time for any of them.

"Cool photo in the paper!" said the boy in the group, with what might have been appreciation, or might have been contempt; Geo couldn't tell.

His feet were heavy, but he wasn't going home until it was done. The steam of the day's heat lifted off the flagstones' smooth surfaces in bands, and the door looked a thousand miles away, only Mr. Stein had seen him coming, somehow, he'd been looking out his own window the way Geo had been looking out of his. It wasn't supposed to work that way, but it did. Mr. Stein was like that.

He opened the door when Geo's hand lifted toward the bell, as if to prevent the dangerous music.

"Hello!" said Mr. Stein, his voice rowdy, loud. But Geo noted how the lines on his forehead, an ocean of waves, a horizon, made it clear he was not feeling well. Maybe he was nauseated, or about to cry. His eyes were large and watery behind the glasses, which he pushed up to rub at the bridge of his nose.

"How may I help you, young neighbor?"

Geo was going to tell him, *Your son hit me.* He had practiced those exact words in his head, with or without the prologues, *He probably didn't mean it,* or *My mother really wants me to tell you,* but in the minute it took to walk to the door, he'd decided just to say it. *Your son hit me.*

"I have something to tell you," he said, unable to go through with his plan. Mr. Stein put the glasses back on his nose. There was an ink stain on the pocket of his button-down shirt. Laundered, maybe sprayed for the stain, but still, it was there, a blue ballpoint ghost. He wondered whether Mr. Stein wrote all day. His own father had calluses where he peeled labels from the machine and adhered them to bottles and boxes of medications. His own father seemed very young, compared to Mr. Stein.

"You do? Well, then, come in," said Mr. Stein. "Would you like some coffee? No, of course not. How about a soda?"

Geo did want a soda. He wanted the shrill sugar sensation in his throat. He wanted to drink instead of speaking. He followed Mr. Stein into the kitchen. Heart-shaped backs on wire chairs, like an ice-cream parlor. He sat down and felt the cold glass of the table under his fingertips.

"It's about your stepdaughter, about Linsey," he said.

"Okay," said Mr. Stein, gulping slightly. Geo paused.

"Did you want that soda? Would you like something?

Some cookies? I don't know what we have . . ." Mr. Stein opened the fridge and left the door balanced on the weight of its own booty: unsalted butter, pickles, fudge sauce, seltzer, and crackers in the door. Geo wondered why anyone would put crackers in the refrigerator. Now Mr. Stein was opening the cabinets, all of them, like undressing, making the kitchen nude for Geo. His back was to the boy. He kept talking.

"You wouldn't want crackers? I think we have some peanut butter. Where do we keep the cookies?"

Geo waited, because he hadn't decided how to say it, he hadn't even planned to say it, but that ocean of forehead changed the subject for him. Finally Mr. Stein was done, and he sat on one of the heart chairs across from Geo with an empty glass in his hand. All the doors were still open.

"Okay," he said. "What would you like to tell me?" He held his hand up to his throat. Mottled, pinkish, soft skin for a man. He needed to shave.

"It may not be important," he said. *He wanted to say, Please keep breathing. Please don't have a heart attack. It may not be important.*

"Okay," said Mr. Stein, again.

"I found this paper—"

The doorbell rang.

"I just thought it was trash—"

The doorbell rang again. Mr. Stein waved his hand at it, as if he could stop the ringing with a swat.

"My mom gave it to the police. But before she did I was looking at it, and I realized—"

"Realized what, Geo?" There was a cheering from outside, or perhaps it was jeering, either way, it was distracting Mr. Stein.

"Goddamn kids!" he snapped. Geo flinched.

Three rings, overlapping.

"Well, I'm not *one hundred percent* sure. But—".

"I want to hear," said Mr. Stein, over the ringing. "Please, but I have to get that."

He picked up an apple pie, still wrapped with blue-tinted plastic, and went to the door. For a minute, Geo just sat, holding the rest of his story under his tongue. Then he went to the door, too, certain his mother had come to get him.

Someone was standing by the door, but Mr. Stein had passed him. He was standing in front of the group of kids on the lawn, holding the pie as if to offer them some.

"That's enough," he said quietly. His face was plum. "You can all go home."

"Man," said the boy, but he picked himself up off the grass.

Tina Sentry was drawing on her friend's arm with a felt-tip marker.

"We're just, like, showing our support," said the friend, without looking up at Mr. Stein.

"I said, go home," said Mr. Stein. He lifted the pie above his head and smashed it on the ground. It made only a small, squishy sound, but his rage was apparent. The pie exploded against the grass and a fat slice of cooked apple splatted on Tina's pen-clutching fist.

"Fine!" she said, and jumped up. The girls dispersed like crows fleeing a tossed stone, cawing contempt and disbelief. They gathered their things and walked toward the sidewalk, leaving candles lit on the lawn.

Geo could smell the cinnamon. He came out on the stoop and stood beside the person who had rung the bell. It was Jordan from Starbucks, with whom he'd shared photographs and ideas, who was on his list of suspects he'd made with Timmy. Geo had seen Jordan walking down the street with a cello case on wheels, standing half in the doorway, a look like drowning on his face. As Mr. Stein returned, Jordan started saying something Geo missed, but he heard the rest, the man's voice bare and almost crying.

"Pardon me," said Mr. Stein, wiping his hands and looking at Jordan quizzically. "They were just so noisy, chattering on, and they were ruining the grass."

Jordan was breathless. He continued as if Mr. Stein hadn't said anything.

"So I need to use your phone, because his wasn't working, because I need to call the police. I have to call them, because he was—" He looked over at Geo, into Geo's eyes, in that aggressive way that hurt, the way kids sometimes looked at him, as if they might read him, as if he had words through his eyes on the back of his skull. Geo looked down.

"He was"—as if Geo didn't know how to spell—"D-E-A-D."

His mother had been walking in the backyard again last night. Toby knew because his father's weight made the floorboards speak when he got up and went to the window. Toby had gone out to the bathroom, which faced the backyard, to see what his father was watching. In the past, once or twice, it had been a raccoon, once a skunk when the local paper had reported a rabid one wandering, and his father told them to stay out of the backyard. But this time it was Mom, pacing, barefoot. He could feel his father watching the same things he was, and last night it had been his mother, wandering the backyard in sweatpants and a moth white shirt that belonged to his father, a button-down he'd worn and left unbuttoned by the back steps when he got home from work. His father was usually meticulous, but this thing with Linsey had thrown him off balance.

When Mom was wandering outside, something was missing, something else, besides Linsey. It was as if the house was part of his mother's body, lungs or arms, attached, integrated, essential to her operation and vice versa. Symbiotic, he thought, imagining his mother as a sucker fish held fast to a shark. His dad thought he was being quiet when he wandered, but Toby could hear it all, the shuffling steps down the stairs, the kiss of the fridge opening, the wine his father poured to the brim of a juice glass, even the drinking. Then there was the click of the oven, a metal spoon stirring something in a metal pan, he thought, strange sounds, until Toby fell asleep.

This morning Toby had risen early, even though Cody was still breathing deeply across the room, his nose whistling occasionally, one leg out of the blankets and vulnerable, hanging over the edge of the bed. His skin glinted like a fish in the silvery light.

Downstairs usually smelled like coffee in the morning, but this morning his father was doing something complicated in the kitchen. There were baking sheets and rolling pins and the warm burnt smell of something buttery baking.

It was going to be the first day of school tomorrow. Linsey wasn't home. He usually remembered about her right when he woke up, but today he'd forgotten, thinking about his new class, about the lunch Mom usually made for him, about the note she usually put in his lunch box, about the things he wouldn't have tomorrow because his mother was so distracted. He hoped his father would take the day off tomorrow, too, because it was going to be a minimum day, early dismissal. He felt odd coming down so early, as if he might bother his father in his private bear mode, hunting, gathering, mumbling, like sleepwalking, owning the house with the rustle of his thick legs in a flannel robe. His dad had never been unkind to him, hardly ever got angry, but he did get that look on his face, he did say, "Oh, I'm disappointed," which was worse for Toby than getting slapped. Linsey's father slapped her, once or twice, she'd told him. Linsey was gone. He felt sorry for himself, like an orphan somehow. Until yesterday, he knew she was coming back for sure—now he didn't know anything.

"You're making pancakes?" Toby guessed.

"Croissants," said his father, with a French accent.

"You can *make* those?" Toby wrinkled his nose. The timer went off, and his father pulled out a baking sheet of hand-rolled flaky half-moons from the oven.

"There's tons of butter in there. Lots of rolling out and chilling of the dough. Just what I needed." He smiled and slid two onto a plate for Toby. "I needed to chill out, and I need to eat butter."

"Did Mom come in yet?" If he said it, he wasn't alone in knowing. He worried she'd move her bed outside, she'd leave them, too.

"She's sleeping. These are amazing with raspberry jam." His father set the whole jar in front of him, and handed him a tiny silver spoon from his mother's special set in the dining room hutch. Why were these out, just for breakfast? They usually only came out at Thanksgiving.

"So, croissants and a candy bar okay for lunch tomorrow?" His dad was grinning. There was a mostly empty wineglass on the counter, the dregs like purple ink.

"Yes," said Toby, relishing this conspiracy.

By afternoon his father was asleep in a chair in the living room. His nose buzzed with snores and Toby wanted to ask for the same sort of attention he'd had this morning. He wanted to feel important, but he didn't want to interrupt what was obviously an important restoration.

His mom was outside with some visitors; his brother had gone somewhere without telling or inviting him. This had grown common over the last few days, and it was a trial and a relief to Toby, separation.

"Um," whispered Toby, to his dad, but then the doorbell rang.

He heard everything, though he hadn't listened on purpose. That was how he thought of it, lately, with all the uproar and so many phone calls and visitors and the strange suspicion that had taken up residence in his house. His mother hadn't checked their room in the past day or two, but he knew she was doing it, prowling through their things and leaving them in the same places, but with the dust disturbed. He didn't mind. It was something like his own listening, his need to know.

It was Geo from Cedar Court at the door; he heard from the living room. He'd always admired his neighbor a little— six months older, so much taller, and always absorbed in strange projects in the backyard. What he admired, maybe, was the way Geo didn't seem to need anyone, didn't bounce around at school like a magnetic particle seeking mutual attractions. Toby knew the boy was different, that Geo wasn't bothered by the same things, that he didn't care about sports

and brought pomegranates or cold asparagus for lunch without worrying about being weird and that his skin was dark
and his family's was light. But Toby was different, too, only
he found ways to be the same—the Boy Scouts, playing soccer. He was fine at the ordinary work of being a boy, but he
was better, somehow, at secret things, at learning from what
people said or didn't say when they thought you might not
hear them.

There was something in the conversation between his
father and Geo that made his neck ache. Odd, perhaps it was
being jealous, or perhaps he thought someone wasn't telling
the whole truth, but then the doorbell rang again, and that
guy Jordan came in and started talking about Mr. Leonard
being dead, and it didn't matter anymore.

"Okay," his father said. "We'll call, don't panic."

Toby couldn't stay secluded another minute. He darted
from the living room to the bottom of the stairs, stomping
three times to sound as if he was descending. He'd seen his
father smash the pie.

"What's going on?" he asked Geo, who stood with his
hands around a glass of 7-Up, as if the pale liquid might
warm him.

"They're calling nine-one-one," said the other boy.

"Nine-one-one is not for fun," said Toby, reflexively.
He'd learned that in kindergarten. There had been so much
talk about the police and the detective that the gloss of the
law was dulled for him recently. They'd called the police for
Linsey; they'd followed the orders and they'd checked and

checked, and still her room was empty, still he had a place in his chest the size of a fist that hurt for not having her back.

"Is Mom still outside?" Toby asked his father, who held up his hand while the call went through. He wanted her to come in. He wanted the family contained.

"My neighbor found another neighbor," he began on the phone, his voice slow. "Can you boys wait in the kitchen? Sorry." He pointed toward the swinging door.

And Jordan ushered them into the kitchen, where Geo looked at Toby and Toby looked at the floor. They stood for a minute like statues afraid of pigeons landing, and then his father stepped back in, his face quiet.

"You need to tell them exactly what happened," said Toby's father, putting his hand on Jordan's shoulder. Jordan was shivering, which was strange, because the room was too warm; the central air never worked well in the kitchen, too many windows.

"That guy Mr. Leonard is dead?" Geo asked. "I liked the music," he said. "He was old, right?"

"Not very," said Toby's father. "Mostly, he was very sick."

"Was it like cancer like Johnny Sentry's grandmother?" Toby had to fill the room with something, with talk, with his voice, because his father wasn't paying attention. He hadn't minded a few days of being invisible, but with Geo here, he couldn't help wanting his father's soft and heavy hand to touch his back, or at least to garner the big brown gaze. He wanted the morning back.

"Or was it something else? Like the flu? Did you know people used to die of the flu?"

"They still do," said Geo. "I guess I'd better get home?" He stepped lightly, strangely silent for such a tall boy. Even he wasn't looking at Toby.

"Is your mom home?" His father walked Geo to the front door. Geo seemed unsettled, and suddenly Toby wanted to talk this over with him, a dead neighbor, something other than his sister, something they could stretch out over the hole of her missingness.

"I've never been in your backyard," said Toby, almost wanting to go, almost wanting to ask for a playdate, as if they were five years old. It was weird, this guy was dead next door, and he wanted to go back with Geo to Cedar Court and check out the stuff he had in his house. To maybe make friends with him. Because it was clear there was something special about the boy, something that maybe made Toby like him, or at least his dad liked him, and his dad had good taste in people. And maybe if he went to Geo's house, he'd stop feeling so muted, so soundless.

"Where's Mom?" Toby asked, though he knew she must still be out back.

"Yes," said Geo, and then he left.

"She's in the backyard with Mrs. Sentry and Timmy," said his father, sighing and leaning on his knees. Toby worried about his dad.

Then the phone rang.

His father's whole body moved at once, a leap, to pull the

receiver off the wall. The kitchen stool behind him tipped onto the floor, and he didn't turn around, just walked into the family room for privacy. Toby watched him go, watched him shut the door, but he didn't move closer, he didn't go into the office to pick up the other phone, and not because he was worried about being caught. He sat and spread raspberry jam on a leftover croissant, which was sweet and light and buttery and so good Toby stuffed his mouth, filling it. He wanted more. He let his father talk without listening, knowing, for the first time, that some things were more important than hearing everything, some things were okay unwitnessed, left alone, that his father would eventually share everything he needed to know.

Toby walked into the backyard.

"I wish I did," said Mrs. Sentry, incongruous, laughing like a strange dog howling.

"Honey!" said Toby's mother.

"Dad says the phone is for you," he said.

Abigail sat up suddenly, spilling her mint iced tea. The glass cracked on the stone step beside the grass.

His father was pushing past him, holding out the phone, which he'd switched to speaker.

"Mrs. Stein?" It was that detective, Mr. Barq, his voice broadcast to the audience of Mrs. Sentry, Geo, Timmy, Toby, his father and mother. "I have news."

DAY FIVE

36 SYCAMORE STREET

It was an absolute humiliation, even if no one knew; on her way to pick up Johnny from his first day of school, Reeva sneezed and wet herself. She was taking Charlie's midlife crisis two-seater BMW to spite him, because yesterday he'd been taking time off, and then this morning he told her he needed to go into the office. After the Steins' yesterday, Reeva had gone to Kings to pick up the repulsive pork chops Charlie liked so much, and apples for apple-onion chutney, the thought of which made her gag, but still, he loved them, and lately, he'd been so loving to her, and she'd imagined they might even cook together, sipping wine. Sure, he had to work, but she felt betrayed, as though he'd offered her himself, at least for a few days, that he'd be here for the first day of school, that she wouldn't have to feel so alone, and then: oh yes, duty calls.

"Honey," he'd told the machine this morning, because Reeva couldn't bear to pick up and talk to him, "I'm sorry, honey, I'm not going to make it for dinner."

Honey, honey, honey. Everyone was abuzz because they'd found Linsey Stein, or Linsey Hart, off in the middle of the country somewhere, Colorado, was it? Tina came home thrilling with the food fight they'd had in front of the Steins' while Reeva was off at Kings—apparently Frank lost it and started flinging pie, and then all the kids at the vigil joined in and they threw fistfuls of Doritos all about until the police came, only they were there because the old music teacher had a stroke or something—it was too much for Reeva. She was glad her daughter was home, instead of camped out on someone's lawn in her too-tight clothing.

Abigail Stein had been, surprisingly, a kind person to talk with. Like showing your opponent your poker hand, Reeva had told her about Jordan. Why had she just let go, after holding her hand so carefully from eyes? Maybe it was the expectation of commerce, after Reeva listened to Abigail's worries. Who wouldn't worry—who wouldn't feel like they'd been dissected for the media, for the neighbors, for everyone and left empty with the girl gone—daughters were part of you, organs, they were still connected in a way that influenced your very breath.

"JeSUS!" she yelled, as she felt the wet warmth, and slapped the hood of his car, as if it were responsible, before going inside to change her pants.

It wasn't as if she was about to be late—she was almost never late, even when she tried, even a hundred years ago, when she used to meet her friend Rhonda for playdates with Steve and Rhonda's son, also named Steve, so they called them Stevemeets and got together in the playground where they both felt overwhelmed, as if raising one child was actually enough work to occupy oneself in addition to a part-time job. Rhonda was habitually late, really late, forty-five minutes minimum late, always making some sweet-and-harried excuse about a last-minute phone call or a problem finding keys, but despite knowing this, week after week, Reeva couldn't make herself get to Wyckoff Playground more than five minutes after their planned rendezvous, even if she dawdled, even if she changed Steve's diaper twice before leaving the house, even if she stopped to get a cup of coffee at the Daily Grind, which was all they had in town before Starbucks.

Before all the babies. Before her body was cut one too many times and her bladder became a pathetic weakling. Just yesterday, she'd made an appointment with her gynecologist, who had told her to come in if she ever decided she might want to "take care of that little problem surgically." Ah, *little problem,* she'd thought, as she held the line for twenty-one minutes before getting a real live person to schedule the appointment. Reeva pulled on a clean pair of jeans, and a pair of underwear that she could only think of as granny pants, cotton, white, stretched past any semblance of youthful joie de vivre; she felt a strange pulling sensation in her hips. Maybe it wasn't just that post-baby problem. Maybe that third episiotomy had never healed, or maybe she had a tumor in there, because her mother had a tumor, her sister had a tumor, maybe this stupid thing with Jordan had pissed off God just enough to make him want to smite her, too, belligerent bastard that he was. The Big C. And she hadn't even had a chance to tell Charlie anything. She was not going to let this make her late to pick up Johnny on his first day.

"Oh, Reeva!" Christine cooed, standing with the flock outside the doors of Wilde Elementary School. "How *are* you?"

She smiled at them, Helena and Andrea and Mazie, and Beth Boris, of all people, wearing an odd red silk suit, as if she'd just come from a wedding where she'd been forced at gunpoint to be a bridesmaid. Beth, who was not part of the Group anymore, whose lipstick was much too plummy for that outfit.

"That suit is really something, Beth," she said. "Really brings out your complexion." She hoped someone knew she meant the spider veins. She was feeling especially mean.

Beth smiled, but she wasn't looking right at Reeva's eyes—she was gazing slightly askew, as if Andrea's ear was very compelling.

"Beth was just telling us how she's sold two units on Gale Street."

Sold two units of what? Reeva wondered. *Crack?* Beth was a stay-at-home mom, for god's sake. She still felt a little jilted, she supposed, though if she thought about it, she was the one who'd soured on Beth first.

"I didn't know you had your broker's license?" said Helena, blessed Helena, who had left her harp in the minivan around the corner on Oak Street; Reeva had seen it on the walk over, angel instrument in a Toyota Sienna.

"Just two months," said Beth. "And almost two million in

sales." She gave Andrea's ear that shit-eating grin. Reeva felt her stomach clamp. Her nose itched, too, and she willed herself not to sneeze, not to even think about sneezing. Reeva Sentry Wets Her Pants, she thought, feeling sorry for herself, feeling pathetic.

"What do you think they could possibly have accomplished in one minimum day?" Helena was clearly trying to change the subject.

"Have you signed up for soccer yet? And Scouts? I was hoping someone would co-mother a troop for Janey with me this year." Mazie wore a trim little gray dress. She had clearly done the going-out-of-business sale at Laura Ashley.

"Oh, look, finally," said Beth, as if she hadn't been reveling in the company. The children were issuing from the building, great hordes of wild things, all energy and flying backpacks. The air smelled of sour milk. Reeva suddenly felt very tired.

Mazie was the first to step away from the group to greet her Janey. They walked together down the sidewalk like girlfriends.

"She really dressed up for pickup," said Beth, pretending this was innocent.

"I know," said Christine. "As if she hadn't spent the morning shopping online and ogling the barista at Starbucks."

Reeva's stomach churned. She couldn't stop the heat from spreading across her cheeks. What did they know?

"Oop," said Christine. "Here's my baby!"

"Wow," said Andrea, even before Christine had fully cleared earshot. "She is really just ballooning. Anyone think we should stage a Weight Watchers intervention?"

"That's not very nice," said Beth, and for once, Reeva agreed. Reeva's hips really hurt. It was somehow a familiar pain, a stretching. Had she been growing a tumor for months?

"Oh, those are mine," said Beth. She stepped out of the cluster and hugged her sons, gathering them to her like long-lost soldiers.

Reeva pulled her day planner from her purse, looking for the little red dots she used to mark her cycle, so she'd know at her annual appointments, so she'd always keep tampons stocked, so she'd understand her weepy moods. She was counting on her fingers. Someone bumped into her left thigh. This was impossible.

"Reeva?" said Helena, stroking her arm as if she were a patient. She felt the bump again, then looked over to see Johnny standing there, waiting for his greeting. "Oh, baby!" Reeva stuffed the book into her purse.

"Crap, Mom, I'm not a baby!" Johnny had stepped away from her, mortified in front of his friends.

"Of course not," she said. Had Johnny said *crap*? Had Helena heard him? Never mind.

"Want to get ice cream at Van Dykes? I think Leland and Mark are going with their mom?" Reeva asked, and then caught her breath. It was an awful recognition. The hip pain, the peeing.

"Yeah," he said, "I guess so." Little man. As they walked

down the sidewalk to the car Johnny was telling her something about reading, but she was watching the twins, Cody and Toby Stein, as they took turns riding their father's back and play-tackling him in the field. They were headed for the shortcut through the woods, to walk home, the way Reeva had walked home with Steve when he was the only one in school. When she hadn't been so worn away by all the work of days. Frank Stein looked old, his wild hair mostly gray. She was too old for this; too old to leapfrog back to Young Motherhood, too old to be pregnant, again.

FLIGHT 808

He was absolutely fine until they were over Winnemucca, Nevada. The woman next to Timmy was gorgeous, olive skin and sea green eyes, and a teal silk blouse on a long plane ride. She was in her third year at Stanford, and Timmy let her attention distract and engage him. They laughed about the lettuce in the for-purchase snack sandwiches, *limp and impotent lettuce*. They exchanged numbers, typing "Woman on Plane" and "Man on Plane" in contacts as though they were in a spy movie.

"I thought it was only trains, you know, the pretend-he-is-someone-you-know bit, so they'll assassinate the wrong man."

"You'd do that? You'd sic them on me?"

"You know, stand by your man," she said. "Sit by your man. You could have typed in 'Sylvia.' My name is Sylvia."

"Okay," said Timmy.

"Okay what?" said Sylvia. "That's where you say your name."

"I was being mysterious, and hoping to avoid the inevitable comment about the diminutive."

"Look," she said. "We're over Winnemucca, Nevada." She pronounced it "Winne-mewka," and pointed to the screen on the seat back, which told them travel speed and location.

"Winnemucca," said Timmy, suddenly nauseated. He excused himself and went to the bathroom to vomit.

Winnemucca. Where they'd found Linsey, trying to hitchhike after her ride dropped her off when she didn't have as much money as he'd hoped. She met him online, a guy going to California, a friend of a friend of a friend, which was enough to infuriate Timmy. She wasn't that dumb, she didn't hate herself that way.

He wiped his mouth with a paper towel but wretched again into the silver bowl. It reminded him of kitchens, of mixing bowls. He was going to work in Berkeley—his uncle had several possibilities lined up, but he didn't want a desk job, he wanted to make something. He'd even be a busboy, but he'd like to be in a kitchen.

When he left, no one had spoken to her yet. It was Barq who found her, following some texts and the friend, whose friend had a friend—he'd found out that her ride was already over the state line in California, but Linsey was left behind. He'd walked home from the Steins' knowing this, and beauty became painful. The early moon, two geese, the locust buds on the tree.

He didn't like the idea of Linsey left behind. The truth was, he'd thought he was being noble, but maybe he was really being stupid. He let her think it, that she loved him more, that they were unequal—that uncountable infinity—that it was hers for him. But really, he loved her more. He knew her time with him would end when she grew out of him—it wasn't just the body, his lust, why he pretended to himself that he needed to let her go. It was because even if she didn't, he thought she needed time to grow up, to become without him, and at the same time, he knew he loved her more, that he had to let go before she left him.

Timmy cleaned off his face. She'd been in a bar in Winnemucca, Nevada, searching for change in an ashtray to try the slot machines. He was disgusted at the thought, at the sudden desperation, but still, she'd been going west, toward him. Why hadn't she just called someone collect? What had she imagined when she arrived? Would they have moved in together? He could smell her hair, he wanted her hips against him. He wouldn't call—he'd let her belong to her family again. He'd let her go. He rinsed his mouth and went back to his seat, to Sylvia.

ABIGAIL

Everything was easier in the light. The streets were clear as they pulled off Route 66 and into the little town where they were supposed to find the dirt road. Barq had a map and handwritten instructions, though the rental car had a navigation system. The police had brought her in, like a criminal, like a runaway, only she wasn't a flight risk, so they'd let her go with a respite worker—a woman who volunteered herself in emergencies. Last night Abigail had called from the airport, and the woman had answered first.

"I'm Lila," she said to Abigail. "Your daughter is lovely. She's helping my boys with the horses."

"With the horses?" It sounded odd, and Abigail pictured a carousel.

"We keep ten of 'em. We're short staffed, so she's helping with feeding and grooming."

It was like a conversation from space. Abigail wanted to know what her daughter's hair looked like, whether she'd had a shower, who were these boys? But the woman was just a volunteer, just a free hotel, just a kindness. Abigail could use to offer the world more kindnesses, she thought. Not cupcakes. She needed to volunteer. Proximity to New York had made her selfish. Or maybe she was selfish all along.

"We've got a new one, a flea-bitten gray, and he really likes her."

A flea-bitten gray? "Can I talk to her?"

"They're out, but they'll be back soon."

Like land of the lost. Abigail signed off, knowing she wouldn't get to talk with Linsey until they arrived, until morning.

They stopped at a tiny general store. Barq wanted coffee, though Abigail just wanted to go, go, go. The woman with a bloody apron behind the meat counter wrote out instructions for her on a slip of butcher paper while Barq sipped, and Abigail climbed back into the car feeling ready, calm, her daughter would be there.

Barq yawned and stretched and she noticed his uneven stubble. She hadn't imagined he'd be a redhead. His hair was faded a bit with age, gone more pinkish. He had a ruddy face and kind eyes. He said "God bless" all the time in person, too; he'd met her in the airport at the transfer in Chicago and he'd known who she was before she knew he was himself. He wasn't just Barq, he was Miles Barq, but she had a hard time calling him Miles. They sat side by side on the plane, each respecting the armrest, so neither could let their elbows down.

"We have to go—" But she said it so quietly he didn't hear her. She left the store and sat in the car revving the engine, because Linsey was out there, or at least someone who was named Linsey, who had looked like Linsey. She honked twice into the quiet. Three times more.

"Sorry," Barq said, getting in. She pulled out so fast he spilled a small splash of coffee onto the lid of his cup. A drop on his lap. Then she calmed. She might have burned him. And she needed Barq right now, even if it didn't seem that way, minute to minute. She needed this man, this hired help, as much as she needed Frank to be at home with the boys, to be Frank, waiting for her with his barrel chest and the slight smell of pickles on his breath. Without her, Frank would serve them salads for breakfast, salads and doughnuts. He required her, in a way Joe never had.

This was why Barq had to come with her. Because alone, she wouldn't have found the house, she'd have driven in circles through the night. Because alone, she wouldn't have been able to stanch the wound of her own sobbing.

The road was so rough, Abigail's teeth hurt.

"It's pretty here," said Barq, gripping the oh-my-gosh handle so she could see how tense he was. "The birches, the cardinals, the stupid scenic deer."

She grinned a little despite herself.

"We used to go up to a house near Lake George. Rented, but it felt like it belonged to us. Once I hit a deer. I don't think my kid ever forgave me—even though the deer ran away, she'd seen it bleeding, and she was about six, right smack in the *Bambi* phase."

"I hate that movie," said Abigail. "And *Snow White,* too. You have a kid?"

"I have three." Barq with three kids. Abigail tried to imagine them, redheads with amber eyes. "I hate the way popcorn kernels stick in your teeth. You're at the movies, and your kids are there, so you have to surreptitiously pick at your teeth and not let them see."

"Oh," said Abigail. "I'd let them see."

"Here," said Barq, his voice as raw as his red eyes. "Turn here." She would've missed the little wooden sign.

The house was closed, even the shades drawn tight, but Abigail had been so certain Linsey would be inside she kept knocking. There was no bell, as if no one ever came to visit. She stepped up on a planter filled with black-eyed Susans, almost all dead, and tried to peer in the top of the door.

"I'll try the windows," said Barq. He fished out a pocket-knife and tried to pry open the double-hung windows in the front, but they were metal, and only bent.

"HELLO!" screamed Abigail, as if whoever was in there was just deaf. The ride she'd accepted had just been a boy. Some twenty-something who had apparently gotten mad that Linsey didn't have that much money, or that Linsey didn't want to sleep with him, when they were this close to California. It was Abigail's own fault, whatever Timmy said, it was because she tried to pry them apart that Linsey went after Timmy, even if Timmy had been at home, hoping to help find her.

Linsey had just left with this ride, this friend of a friend, or come to him, or however she got here, there had obviously been some deception, and Abigail, sitting down on the planter and starting to sob, knew it was her own fault, because she'd made her daughter break up with Timmy, because she'd been so worried about being left in the most ordinary way—college—she hadn't had time to notice what was going on right in front of her.

"There are tire tracks," said Barq, rubbing his toe on the grass like a bear tracker.

"I get no signal here." Now he was holding up his phone.

Horses shuffled like shadows in a paddock behind the house. There was frost on the grass. It was four in the morning.

"This isn't the house!" said Barq. He took her hand and they ran like children down the dirt track until a farmhouse popped out of the dry landscape like a desert flower.

"Welcome," said Lila, opening the door wide. "I've just put on coffee." She wore a plaid shirt and jeans and Abigail could see her collecting eggs and rounding up cattle and she felt ridiculous in her clothes, ridiculous in her body, this stranger who had given her daughter a roof was full and flesh and helpful.

"I get it," she said. "One of my boys left last year—he didn't go far, just to work in Vail at a ski place—a ski place! He came home on his own, but I get it. They grow up, but they're always babies. Come in."

"Thank you," said Abigail, looking past the woman into the house. She wanted to see Linsey, she wanted to leave.

She was weeping now, fully weeping, crying for her daughter, who she'd expected to have in her arms now like a baby. Only Linsey hadn't been a baby for so long, even when she let Abigail brush her hair, even when she let Abigail straighten the prom dress she wore when she went as Timmy's date her junior year, and Abigail had wished she hadn't shown so much cleavage, but had only said, *You're so beautiful,* and Linsey had given her that awful embarrassed look, even then, Linsey hadn't been her baby for so long. Abigail had been the needy one, the negative part of the equation.

"Abby." Now Barq was holding her, turning her forward. It was okay for him to call her Abby.

"God bless," he whispered.

Her impossibly tall daughter was walking down the hallway, wearing someone else's pajamas, someone's old blue terry-cloth robe, holding her arms around herself. She had an odd, deep purple bruise on her cheekbone. Oval, like a thumbprint. She shined. Abigail pulled free of Barq, rushed down the hallway, because Linsey was waiting for her mother the way she'd waited after kindergarten, holding herself together, waiting to be collected.

DAY TEN

DAY TEN

22 COTTAGE PLACE

Geo's photo of the vigil—before the pie—had made the front page of the *Bergen Record*. Tina Sentry's face was eerily lit with candlelight, and a boy was laughing behind her. It ran with an article about how the private investigator had tracked Linsey down more than halfway to California, and the headline said "Girl Gone Missing Coming Home." Geo knew there were other possible headlines, and luck made this one right. He wanted to be like the PI, someone who brought people together again. He wondered what it had felt like to run away from the plan, to escape the ordinary possibilities—though he was glad she was coming back, was going on to college, was in the time line intended for her. He thought about how Timmy had helped him sort through photographs, how people choosing to love other people was so much riskier than the requisite love of family.

Mrs. Sentry was sitting in the metal chair beside her husband, her hands wrapped through his with the determination of a dowager holding her purse on the subway. Mr. Sentry was unfamiliar to Geo, just the man in a dark blue suit with weary eyes. Mrs. Sentry's face was oddly sweet, open in a way he hadn't seen before. Perhaps the music opened her. Geo could tell it called to Mr. Sentry, who might not weep, but clearly wanted weeping. Geo's parents held his hands, one on either side, as though they'd known Mr. Leonard well. He wished he had his camera. The Sentry children were at school, only a smattering of other kids sat in seats performing their rituals of distraction—nose rubbing, jittery legs—he thought it would have pleased Mr. Leonard, students at his last recital.

Jordan House played the music without a hint of anxiety, without losing his way. Geo felt the gift of each movement as Jordan's bow etched the notes into the air. Geo felt him. The strange apricot and amber smell of the old man, the smooth and brittle skin, the passion, the great size of it, the density of pleasure and loss made palatable, made comprehensible.

His father leaned toward Linsey Hart's stepfather in the way a friend might, their shoulders gossiping like birds on a wire. Jordan held them all with the music. The pianist was a lovely woman in her forties, and she seemed to love Jordan's notes with her own. Jordan, rough at the edges to Geo, out of place in the ordinary world, fit when he was playing.

And this was the right word for it, "playing," the way children played, making patterns and designs. It was exactly the kind of work Geo needed to do.

Geo took photographs of Jordan as he went door-to-door with invitations to the service, just as Mr. Leonard had asked him. Jordan handed out the little cards printed up at Kinko's: *Please honor the passing of Mr. Amadeus Leonard from this world by attending a service. Music and refreshments.*

Jordan told him it was supposed to be like a party, that Mr. Leonard had said, "I want them to eat." As instructed, Jordan and Geo taped lollipops to each invitation. At some of the houses he'd just stuck them in the mailbox.

They all knew the story now. She'd gone west with some guy, hoping to see her boyfriend when he got to California. Geo had read it, *California,* but by the time he tried to tell, she was found. This didn't bother him as much as the fact that no one wanted the tracing he'd made of the note, so he felt compelled to keep it in his box of trimmed-up photo faces. He texted Timmy, but by the time Timmy read the text, Abigail was on her way. When Timmy's plane landed, Geo got a text back, *You got there first.*

People were strange with ideas—there was talk of a rape, but then he heard she wasn't pressing charges against anyone— that nothing had happened except that she'd been dropped off partway to California, without money. Just a mistake. Just luck that she was unharmed. A youthful indiscretion. But it was no such thing; it was the desire to be missing, if only for a day or two—a need Geo recognized, to walk on the edge so someone would grab you back again before you fell.

Geo stood on the sidewalk while Jordan took the invitation to the Sentrys' house. Reeva's daughter, Tina, had answered their door. She wore a miniskirt and she had Reeva's eyes.

"Hey," she said to Jordan. "I know you."

"I work at Starbucks," he said.

"That's all?" She was rubbing the door handle. It made Geo's lungs hurt, the way she wound herself around.

"This is for your parents," Jordan said.

"Ooo, a lollipop," she said, still flirting.

"I think you'll be in school," he said.

"Who's that?" asked Reeva, coming down the stairs. Jordan turned quickly and joined Geo out on the sidewalk.

"No one," said Reeva's daughter, and her door closed behind them both.

They clapped between movements, which showed how little they knew of music. Geo knew you were supposed to wait. Still, Jordan smiled at the pianist, because it was sweet. Because it meant they wanted to appreciate Mr. Leonard now as they never had when he was living.

Mr. Leonard had left his house to the Musical Society in town, stipulating that they should start a music school if they had the funds. There was even some money for the project.

Linsey Hart's mother, Abigail, was notably absent. Geo could tell her husband's hand ached for hers, that he was pulled into the same longing Mr. Leonard was calling out, sweet longing. She was staying for a few more days at Cornell, everyone had seen them going, just the two of them in the wagon, riding low with a trunk in the back and a bike on the roof. Linsey held her arm out to test the current of the air, riding the wind like a child. Geo had been helping Jordan lug Mr. Leonard's garbage out to the curb. Jordan was going to give Geo music lessons—maybe even teach him to write his own music for movies. He'd asked, and Jordan told him Mr. Leonard had said the symphony wasn't for Linsey, but of course it was for her as well. And in the end, there was the music, calling out secrets and truths. There will always be sorrow, the composer told his students and his neighbors, and it is only a choice of sharing it this way, or letting it go.

ACKNOWLEDGMENTS

Thank you to the exquisite queens of the written word Jen Carlson and Emilia Pisani, and to the good folk of S&S who work to make a beautiful book and bring it out into the world, including Jennifer Bergstrom, John Paul Jones, Chris Sergio, Stephanie DeLuca, and Sally Franklin.

Thank you to my friends and writing students, including Cindy Starr, Lisa Roe, Suzanne Samuels, Maria Oskwarek, Joanne Nesi, Ardith Toomey, Lisa Summers, Phyllis Rosenthal, Annie Cami, Lisa Williamson, Kris Linton, Jane Paterson, and Sandy Desmond. Thank you to brilliant first reader Veera Hiranandani. Thanks to the folks at Saddle Ridge Riding Center, who fill our days with horsey happiness. Sammy gave me the original title. Thank you to the Gross, Rosenberg, Herman, Colao, and Rose clans and all their branches and twigs.

And thank you to my family: Jacob, Carina, Josh, you bring me cosmic joy.

GALLERY READERS GROUP GUIDE

WHEN SHE WAS GONE

GWENDOLEN GROSS

INTRODUCTION

When seventeen-year-old Linsey Hart goes missing just days before her scheduled departure for college, a typically quiet New Jersey neighborhood is left peeking out windows and into backyards for clues. There's Linsey's mother, Abigail, whose door-to-door searching makes her social outcast status painfully obvious; stay-at-home mom Reeva, whose primary concern is covering up the affair she's been having with the Starbucks barista; Mr. Leonard, a reclusive retired piano teacher—and the last person to see Linsey alive; George, an eleven-year-old gifted loner who is determined to find out what happened to Linsey; and Timmy, Linsey's ex-boyfriend, who is left grieving as he embarks on his own college career.

With a sly humor and ultimate optimism, the stories of this small town converge in unexpected ways, painting a complex and illuminating portrait of a community moved by grief, devoured by suspicion, and consumed by secrecy.

DISCUSSION QUESTIONS

1. The neighborhood in the novel is one built on secrets; every character seems to have a secret to hide. How do the secrets the characters hold influence their relationships with others?

2. Through her memories, we learn that the loss of their two-week-old son is what drives Abigail into depression and her and Joe apart. Though her interactions with Joe are limited, what information do you gather about him?

3. Prior to her disappearance, how is Linsey viewed by those around her: Her mom? Her brothers? Reeva? Timmy? Which of these people do you think Linsey would feel viewed her in the way she wanted to be viewed?

4. Reeva and Jordan's affair is a source of excitement and guilt for Reeva. What first attracts her to Jordan, despite his disheveled appearance and home? How does her revelation about Jordan's age cause her to see their tryst in a new light?

5. On pages 77–78, we get a glimpse of the Group, Reeva's gaggle of housewives who come together to discuss play-dates and car pool logistics—or, really, to trade gossip and make passive-aggressive comments about one another. How would you describe the women in the group? Why do you think Reeva invites them into her home; why do you think she cares so much what they think?

6. What did you learn about Charlie and Reeva on the day Charlie stays home from work (pg. 205–207)? What do Reeva's internal thoughts about Charlie reveal about their relationship and about herself?

7. Compare and contrast Toby's and Cody's reactions to Linsey's disappearance. Do you think one of them deals with his feelings better than the other?

8. "In this town, people were very small about difference, about seeking otherness" (pg. 67). In this passage, Timmy reflects on how Geo is treated by the neighborhood as compared to how he might be treated in a larger-minded, more accepting place. Are there characters in the novel other than Geo who you feel are mistreated by the community because of their "otherness"?

9. On page 50, Geo references "Mending Wall," a poem by Robert Frost, as he considers the two fences between his property and the Steins'. Read the poem, found at

http://www.bartleby.com/104/64.html, and consider its meaning. Do you see any connection between Frost's poem and the neighborhood in the novel? Is there a particular line that resonates with you, or that you feel reflects a particular character?

10. Abigail and Timmy avoid each other for days after Linsey's disappearance. Why do you think that is; what do you think they were feeling that kept them from confronting each other? Guilt? Fear? A different emotion? Ultimately, what leads Timmy to finally walk up to Abigail's doorstep and talk with her?

11. When Abigail is finally reunited with her lost daughter, Linsey is described as "waiting for her mother the way she'd waited after kindergarten, holding herself together, waiting to be collected" (pg. 266). As Abigail rushes to "collect" her, what emotions do you think she is feeling? How do you suspect Linsey has changed from the beginning of her journey? How has Abigail changed?

12. Jordan and Mr. Leonard's unlikely friendship is based on their mutual love of music. Mr. Leonard offers Jordan his musical mentorship; what does Jordan offer him in return? How do the themes of music—listening and making—weigh in the novel?

13. The novel both opens and closes with Mr. Leonard—opening on a chapter from his perspective, and closing at his memorial service. Why do you think the author chose Mr. Leonard as the character holding the novel together in this way?

14. Throughout the novel, a narrator offers readers a detailed glimpse into each of the characters' houses. What do you think their homes say about them? Was there a particular home that you felt reflected the character who lived within it the most?

READING GROUP ENHANCERS

1. Geo's photographs of those around him gives him a view of the neighborhood others do not have; through photography and collage-making, he can decipher the "sameness and difference" others miss (pg. 45). Try to see things from Geo's point of view: Before your book club discussion, ask each member to carry a camera with them for a day, taking pictures of the everyday places and people they might usually overlook. Then, at your discussion, consider the photographs: What do you see? Does anything in the pictures surprise you?

2. As Reeva prepares her home for the Group to arrive, she recalls Charlotte Perkins Gilman's short story *The Yellow Wallpaper,* the tale of a woman who slowly goes mad while she's locked in an upstairs bedroom by her husband. Find a copy of this short story, either online or in your local bookstore or library, and give it a read. Do you see any common themes in *The Yellow Wallpaper* and *When She Was Gone*? Does the narrator in the short story share any characteristics with the women narrators in the novel?

3. Two coffee shops are mentioned in the novel: the notorious Starbucks where Jordan works, and the Daily Grind. Do you have a favorite coffee shop in your town? Consider holding your book club discussion there for a change of scenery.

Gwendolen Gross is the author of multiple critically acclaimed novels. To learn more about Gwendolen and her books, visit her websites at www.gwendolengross.com and www.whenshewasgone.com or follow her on Twitter @GwendolenGross